LEFT BEHIND®

>THE KIDS<

Jerry B. Jenkins

Tim LaHaye

WITH CHRIS FABRY

TYNDALE HOUSE PUBLISHERS, INC.
WHEATON, ILLINOIS

DEDICATION

To Reagan Michael

Visit Tyndale's exciting Web site at www.tyndale.com

Discover the latest Left Behind news at www.leftbehind.com

Published in association with the literary agency of Alive Communications, Inc., 7680 Goddard Street, Suite 200, Colorado Springs, CO 80920.

Edited by Curtis H. C. Lundgren

ISBN 0-8423-4331-8

Printed in the United States of America

08 07 06 05 04 03 02 01 00
9 8 7 6 5 4 3 2 1

Table of Contents

What's Gone On Before

JUDD Thompson Jr. and his friends are in the middle of the adventure of a lifetime. After hearing a report about their friends in Israel, Judd and Ryan Daley hurry to the Holy Land to discover their fate. Judd is jailed by the Global Community. Ryan helps him escape, but the two are suspicious of their pilot, Taylor Graham.

After the kids' new friends, Darrion Stahley and her mother, leave without a trace, Vicki Byrne and Lionel Washington get busy with a new edition of the *Underground*. The memorial service for their beloved pastor, Bruce Barnes, is set for Sunday. They secretly invite everyone at school to hear what Bruce believed will happen next.

As the Young Trib Force gathers on the night before the memorial service, they meet the famous Rabbi Tsion Ben-Judah.

Now the future for the kids is uncertain. Who will show up at the memorial service?

Will the pilot, Taylor Graham, lead the Global Community to them? What will they do without Bruce?

Join the kids as they struggle to make right choices as the world falls apart around them.

ONE
Caught

JUDD Thompson Jr. held his breath. The head of the Tribulation Force was about to ask the rabbi to become their new spiritual leader. The other kids joined Judd to listen outside the door. The Trib Force was meeting with a man Nicolae Carpathia hated. Judd couldn't help thinking about the danger.

Rayford Steele, Nicolae Carpathia's pilot, led the rabbi into the room. Rayford looked at Judd and smiled, then left the door slightly ajar. The other kids crowded around.

"Tsion, my brother," Rayford said, "we would like to ask you to join our little core group of believers. We're not asking for an immediate decision, but we need a leader, someone to replace Bruce."

As Judd watched, Tsion rose and placed his hands atop the table. The man was only in his forties, but to Judd he looked much older. The rabbi spoke with a shaky voice.

"My dear brothers and sisters in Christ," Tsion said, "I am honored and grateful to God for saving my life. We must pray for those who helped me escape.

"I am sad, but I see the hand of God Almighty guiding me. I am right where he wants me. I need no time to think it over. I have prayed already. I will accept your offer to become a member of the Tribulation Force."

Judd saw tears in the eyes of the other group members as Tsion said, "I cannot promise to replace Bruce Barnes, but I will dedicate the rest of my life to sharing the gospel of Jesus Christ, my Messiah."

With that, the man seemed to collapse in his chair, and the others in the room knelt.

"Come on," Judd whispered.

"I knew he'd accept," Ryan said when the kids returned to the living room, "but how do you pronounce his name?"

"Just say 'Zion,' " Chaya said. "That's pretty close in English."

"Do you think he'll teach us like Bruce did?" Lionel said.

"I don't think we'll have much contact with him," Judd said. "After the memorial service tomorrow, they'll probably keep him hidden."

Lionel awoke Sunday morning knowing it might be the toughest day of his life. The excitement and tension of the past week had kept him from thinking much about Bruce. But now, on the day they would say good-bye, he felt a pain deep in his chest.

There had been no funeral for Lionel's family. On the morning of the disappearances, he had discovered only the clothes of his parents and siblings. His older sister, Clarice, had been reading her Bible. His mother had been kneeling in prayer. Lionel still wondered if she had been praying for him at the moment she vanished. He felt so guilty for being left behind. He had known the truth but had not acted on it.

But today was different. Unlike his family, the body of Pastor Bruce Barnes would be there. He could see it. Touch it.

Lionel thought back to his first meeting with Bruce. He had felt so alone that day. The man let them watch a video that explained what had happened. Then Bruce told his own story. God had Lionel's attention. He finally understood that being a Christian wasn't following a set of rules or doing certain things. It had to do with his heart.

And his heart ached. It was hard to lose every member of his family. He had taken them for granted, his mom and dad especially. But losing Bruce was different. When Bruce spoke of spiritual things, Lionel really listened. Now Bruce was gone. Lionel wondered if he would ever have another teacher like him.

Vicki and Chaya stayed at Loretta's house overnight. The next morning they kept to themselves as the adults got ready for the morning service.

"I need a favor," Chaya said. "My mother's funeral is this afternoon as well. You know my dad doesn't want me there, but I have to go."

Vicki placed her hand on Chaya's shoulder. "You don't have to say anything more," Vicki said. "I'll go with you."

Two hours before Bruce Barnes's service began, the Young Trib Force met at New Hope Village Church. Judd prayed, "Give us wisdom and help us do what's right."

Judd welcomed John and Mark. The two

cousins quickly updated the group. John was off to college in a few days. Mark had rebounded from his scrape with death in the militia. "I'm not going back to school," he said. "I'd like to help you guys any way I can."

"We can use it," Judd said. He looked at the kids gravely. "This is not how Bruce planned it," he said. "I'm sure he wanted to live until the Glorious Appearing of Christ. But that won't happen now. Nobody elected me leader, so I'm open to a vote—"

"We don't need that," Lionel interrupted. "You go ahead."

The others agreed.

"I haven't done things perfectly," Judd said. "When Ryan and I went to Israel with that pilot, Taylor Graham, we may have led the Global Community straight to us.

"And I've done other stupid things. More than once, I was mad at Bruce because I thought he was treating us like kids. Now I know he just cared."

Judd saw Vicki wipe her eyes, and he looked away. He had to hold it together until the service.

"For some reason, God let this happen to Bruce," he continued. "And one of the things Bruce told us was that when bad things happen, they will either turn you away from

God or draw you closer to him. You'll run away or become more committed."

"I want to be more committed," Ryan said.

"Me too," Lionel said.

"Then we have to face the facts," Judd said. "First, Bruce is gone and we need to grieve for him. It's OK to cry. In fact, it's good. Second, we're hopefully going to see a lot of people from school here. The *Underground* got the word out. But a few might not be here to mourn."

"You mean spies?" Lionel said.

"Or worse," Judd said. "I wouldn't be surprised if there were some people from the administration here to see if they can catch somebody."

"I hope they do come," Vicki said. "They need to hear it like everybody else."

"But we still have to be careful," Judd said. "You know the school will clamp down hard if they can figure out who put the last issue of the *Underground* together."

"I think we ought to spread out during the service," Lionel said.

"Good idea," Vicki said. "That way they won't see us together."

Judd brought the group up to date on Buck and Tsion. "Buck told me about their drive across the desert," he said. "They were in an old bus. Once a Global Community officer searched the bus while Buck was stopped. Buck thought Tsion was sleeping in the back, but the officer didn't find him."

"Where was he?" Ryan said.

"Buck found him after the officer left," Judd said. "Tsion said he had to go to the bathroom, so when the bus stopped he found some bushes by the road."

"God works in mysterious ways," Lionel said. Everyone laughed.

"He does," Judd said. "At one checkpoint a guard actually found the rabbi hiding."

"Did they arrest him?" Lionel said.

"No," Judd said. "Tsion was praying God would blind the guard or make him careless, but the man shined a flashlight in Tsion's face and grabbed him by the shirt. The guard said, 'You had better be who I think you are, or you are a dead man.' "

The kids stared at Judd.

"Finally, the rabbi told him his name. The guard said, 'Pray as you have never prayed before that my report will be believed.' Then he said a blessing and walked off the bus."

"Incredible," Lionel said.

"If that's not God, I don't know what is," Ryan said, "but what happened when they got to the airport? That's where we lost the transmission."

Judd explained that he and Ryan had picked up a radio report of the chase on their way back from Israel.

"There were so many squad cars at the roadblock," Judd said, "that Buck and Tsion set the bus on fire and ran. Buck got shot in the foot, but they were able to take off and get back home safely."

As the service grew near, Judd suggested they meet afterward in the same room. Everyone agreed. Judd then asked Chaya to lead the group in a brief Bible study. She took them to several passages in Luke and John that spoke of the cost of following Jesus.

"The Scriptures are clear," Chaya said. "A life of following God is not easy, but when we give our lives to him, he gives us the power to live and the promise of eternal life. What more could we need?"

Vicki couldn't believe her eyes when she looked outside. The service was still a half hour away, but the parking lot was full and cars lined the street as far as she could see. Inside, the crowd sat in silence, staring at the casket or looking at their programs. Many cried, but no one sobbed. Vicki hoped she wouldn't either.

She sat at the end of a pew toward the front. She stared at the closed casket. She had been to only a couple of funerals, and she hadn't paid much attention.

She opened the program and read the contents. A verse on the back read, "I know that my Redeemer lives."

She had known Bruce since the day of the disappearances. She had lived under his roof and had even been adopted by him. And yet, she felt there were many things she didn't know. The program listed his date of birth, and she realized she had never thought to ask how old he was. Vicki did the math in her head. "Bruce was preceded by his wife, a daughter, and two sons, who were raptured with the church," the program read. Their names were listed.

Several times Vicki looked up from the page to keep from crying. She spotted Buck and Chloe Williams behind her near Rayford Steele's wife, Amanda. Rayford would be on the platform soon, talking about Bruce. If there was anyone who could give a tribute to Bruce and speak the message Bruce would want these people to hear, it was Rayford.

Loretta entered and sat near the back. It

took Vicki a second look to realize she was with Rabbi Ben-Judah.

The other members of the Young Trib Force were scattered throughout the crowd. She thought she would make it without crying until she spotted Ryan. He was in the front row of the balcony, his eyes red. He waved and tried to smile, then buried his face in his hands.

At ten o'clock Ryan saw Rayford Steele walk through a door at the side of the platform. Another elder stepped to the pulpit and asked everyone to stand. He led them in singing two hymns. Ryan couldn't get the words out.

Vicki smiled when she remembered Bruce's singing. Bruce had admitted he couldn't sing well, but that didn't stop him from belting out what he called a "joyful noise" during congregational songs. At the end of one service he had leaned over to Vicki and said, "What I lack in tone, I make up for in volume."

She smiled again as the songs ended. The elder told the congregation there would be no offering or announcements, just the tribute to Bruce. "Our speaker this morning is Elder Rayford Steele. He knew Bruce as well as any of us."

Judd sat in the back. Bruce had died more than a week earlier, but it still didn't feel real. Hearing Rayford's voice, calm and in control, eased the pain a bit.

Rayford opened his notes and welcomed everyone. "I need to tell you I'm not a preacher," he began. "I am here because I loved Bruce. And since he left his notes behind, I will, in a small way, speak for him today."

Judd imagined himself at the pulpit, wondering what he would say, when an old woman and a young boy walked in. The woman wore dark sunglasses. Judd stood and offered them his seat.

"I want to tell you how I first met Bruce," Rayford was saying, "because I know that many of you met him in much the same way. We were in the greatest crisis of our lives, and Bruce was there to help."

Judd moved to the back of the sanctuary, but people were standing shoulder to shoulder from the last pew to the back wall. He looked into the balcony and saw a space near the sound booth.

Ryan had heard Rayford's story before. He had been best friends with Rayford's son, Raymie. Ryan had even been at their house once when Mrs. Steele had talked about the rapture of the church with her husband.

Rayford explained that he had called the church when he discovered his wife and son were missing. Then he met Bruce and saw the video the former pastor had left behind.

"If you had asked people five minutes before the Rapture what Christians taught about God and heaven," Rayford said, "nine in ten would have said to live a good life, do the best you can, be kind, and hope for the best. It sounded good, but it was wrong! The Bible says our good deeds are worthless. We have all sinned. All of us are worthy of the punishment of death."

Ryan looked around the room and saw a lot of new faces. The *Underground* had done a good job of bringing people in. Now it was Rayford's turn to give them the message.

"I would fail Bruce if I didn't say this," Rayford said. "Jesus has paid the penalty. The work has been done. We can't earn our salvation; it's a gift from God."

Judd exited through the back doors and swiftly made his way to the balcony stairs. The overhead speakers carried Rayford's voice throughout the building.

Judd stopped and listened as Rayford said, "If I can get through this, I would like to speak directly to Bruce. You all know that the body is dead. But Bruce, we thank you. We envy you. We know you are with Christ. And we confess we don't like it that you're gone. We miss you. But we pledge to carry on. We will study, and this church will be a lighthouse for the glory of God."

Tears in his eyes, Judd put his hand on the railing. As he did, someone grabbed his arm roughly and turned him around. The man clamped his hand over Judd's mouth and leaned close.

"Don't make a sound," Taylor Graham whispered. "You're coming with me."

TWO

Rayford's Message

VICKI hung on every word. Rayford was about to preach the very sermon Bruce would have given. "But before I do that, I want to give you a chance to say something in memory of our brother."

Vicki looked around. No one moved. Finally, she heard a voice from the back. Loretta stood and described how she had worked with Bruce since the disappearances. She challenged people to give their lives to Christ as Bruce did, then she broke down. The man next to her gently put his arm around her.

People around Vicki wept. Loretta was crying. Vicki wanted to stand and say something, but she felt nervous. Would anyone care what she thought about Bruce? Finally, she knew if she didn't say something, her heart would break. She stood.

Taylor Graham hustled Judd through the front door and around the side of the church. Judd tried to pull away, but the pilot was strong. Judd looked for Global Community officers or a squad car. Two blocks from the church, Graham found his car, unlocked the passenger side, and pulled Judd in after him.

Vicki shook, but she knew what she was doing was right.

"I've done some bad things in my life," Vicki said. "When my family disappeared, I thought I hadn't been good enough. Then I met Bruce, and I heard the message.

"He was always kind, and it never bothered him that I asked a lot of questions. When I got sent to a detention center, he visited me. When I heard someone wanted to adopt me and make me his daughter, I couldn't imagine who. But I should have known."

Vicki's voice trembled. She pushed her hair behind an ear and bit her lip.

"I can't tell you how much Bruce helped

me understand God's love," Vicki continued. "Mr. Steele is right. God loved us enough to want to adopt us into his family, even when we didn't deserve it. That's what Bruce did for me, and I'll always love him for it."

Vicki scanned the crowd. Some wiped their eyes. Others nodded. Everyone looked at her.

"Don't let this day go to waste," Vicki said. "If you don't know God, ask him to forgive you today and become his child. You'll never regret it."

Vicki sat and bowed her head. From all over the sanctuary people stood and told what Bruce meant to them. After more than an hour, Rayford said they could take one more person before a brief break.

Vicki heard a voice with a thick accent behind her. "You do not know me," Tsion Ben-Judah said. "Many Christian leaders around the globe knew your pastor, learned from him, and were brought closer to Christ because of him. My prayer for you is that you would continue his ministry and his memory, that you would, as the Scriptures say, 'not grow weary in doing good.' "

At Rayford's request, Vicki and the congregation stood and stretched. "We're long past our normal closing time," he said, "so I'd like to excuse any who need to leave."

As Rayford backed away from the pulpit, everyone sat down and looked at him. Someone giggled, then another, and a few more. Rayford smiled, shrugged, and returned to the pulpit.

"I guess there are things more important in this life than personal comfort, aren't there?" he said. Vicki heard a few amens. Rayford opened his Bible and Bruce's notes.

A thousand thoughts flashed through Judd's mind as Taylor Graham drove in silence. Was Graham turning him over to the hands of the North American Global Community? Was he out for revenge for Judd and Ryan's escape? Judd had always been able to think quickly. Now he didn't know what to say or do.

Graham turned into the forest preserve that led to the Stahley property.

They wound along the access road and to the edge of the woods. Graham stopped the car, flipped on a gadget on his dashboard, then sped into a clearing. The pilot activated a remote control device, and the side of the hill opened. Graham drove into the secret plane hangar and punched the door closed.

"Why didn't you do that the first time we came here?" Judd said.

"Ground was wet," Graham said. "The tracks would have led them right to us." The pilot got out of the car. "Follow me," he said.

Ryan listened carefully as Rayford outlined his message. The words were Bruce's, written on an airplane while returning from a trip. Some of the things Bruce wrote sounded spooky.

Rayford said, "Bruce writes, 'I was ill all night last night and feel not much better today. I was warned about viruses, despite all my shots. I can't complain. I have traveled to many countries without problem. God has been with me. If I'm not better upon my return, I'll get checked out.'

"This message is particularly urgent, because he was convinced we are at the end of the time of peace. Bruce writes, 'If I am right, we must prepare for the next prediction: The Red Horse of the Apocalypse.'"

I don't like the sound of this, Ryan thought.

Rayford continued reading from Bruce's writing. " 'Revelation 6:3-4 predicts what I believe is a global war. It will likely become known as World War III. This will immediately usher in the next two horses of the apocalypse, the black horse of plague and famine, and the pale horse of death.' "

Ryan watched Rayford look up from his notes. "Do any of you find this as astounding as I do?" Rayford asked.

Ryan nodded. *It's happening right now!* he thought.

"This was written just before or just after the first bomb was dropped in our global war. I don't know about you, but I want to listen to a man like this."

Ryan quickly thumbed through his Bible as Rayford read from Revelation 6.

" 'And I looked up and saw a horse whose color was pale green like a corpse. And Death was the name of its rider, who was followed around by the Grave. They were given authority over one-fourth of the earth, to kill with the sword and famine and disease and wild animals.'

"Bruce says, 'I'll admit I don't know what the wild animals refer to,'" Rayford continued. "'They could be real animals or perhaps the weapons used by the Antichrist and his enemies. Whatever it means, one-fourth of the world's population will be wiped out. Of the quarter of the earth's population that will perish, surely many, many of these will be tribulation saints.' "

Ryan shuddered. *A fourth of all the people on earth. Will I be one of them?*

Judd sat and Taylor Graham pulled a chair near him. The pilot shook his head and frowned. "You guys gave me the slip in Indy," he said. "Got me in big trouble."

Judd gritted his teeth. "You sold us out," he said.

"Why do you say that?"

"Never mind why," Judd said. "Do you admit it?"

Graham looked at the floor. "There's a lot you don't know," he said. "A lot I still can't tell you. I guess you deserve to hear my side."

Vicki felt lost. The meeting was a tornado of emotion. And now she was listening to Mr. Steele talk about the first four of seven Seal Judgments. She tried to focus.

Thankfully, Mr. Steele asked for a five-minute break. "We'll meet back here at one o'clock. Then I'll make us all aware of what we have to look forward to within the next few weeks."

Vicki looked for Judd in the front hallway but couldn't find him. Lionel slipped in beside her.

"Pretty intense, huh?" Lionel said.

"Imagine sitting in there and not knowing

any of those predictions from the Bible," Vicki said. "You'd have to believe this is true."

"It might be too scary," Lionel said. "People can shut out what they don't want to hear."

"Mr. Steele is telling us stuff I haven't heard yet," Vicki said. "And I don't get the four horses and the seven seals."

Lionel leaned against the wall as some people crowded by, eager to get back into the service before Rayford began again.

"I talked with Chaya yesterday," Lionel said. "She's got it down. The four horsemen are the first four judgments from God. The red horse is the start of the war, then the rest of them—famine, plague, and death—happen right after. Bruce thinks we're right in line for numbers five, six, and seven."

"And then Jesus comes back?" Vicki said.

"No," Lionel said. "There are two more seven-part judgments after this one." Lionel frowned. "I guess that's why they call it the Tribulation. There's a lot of trouble ahead."

Vicki held up a hand. "Speaking of trouble," she said.

"What is it?"

Vicki nodded toward the stairs. Coming towards them was the principal of Nicolae High, Mrs. Jenness.

Before Taylor Graham could speak again, Judd took over. "You sold us out," Judd said. "You were going to give us over to the Global Community."

"Is that why you took off?" Graham said. "Darrion tipped you off on the phone?"

Judd didn't answer.

"I thought I could trust you guys," Graham said. "That whole thing with Ryan being sick was a big act."

"You thought you could trust *us?!*" Judd yelled. "If we'd stayed with you, the GC would have been all over us."

"You don't understand. If you'd stayed with me, I could have pointed them away from you. It's too late for that now."

"I thought you were working with the GC," Judd said. "They're after us."

"No, they're after *you,*" Graham said. "They're interested in Ryan, but only because he can lead them to you."

"We shouldn't be seen together," Lionel said.

Vicki was thinking the same thing, but it was too late now. Mrs. Jenness spotted Vicki and Lionel and came directly toward them. She pursed her lips and looked down.

"I know we've had our differences," Mrs. Jenness said, "but I'm genuinely sorry for your loss."

"Thank you," Vicki said.

"My guess was that the people who wrote the *Underground* newspaper would be here today," Mrs. Jenness said, looking suspiciously at Vicki.

"Could be," Vicki said. "But there are an awful lot of people from the school here."

Mrs. Jenness frowned. "I have to go," she said. "The memorial service was very . . . enlightening." She fixed her stare on Lionel. "You're Lionel Washington, aren't you?"

Vicki didn't know Mrs. Jenness even knew Lionel's name, and it startled her.

"Yes, ma'am," Lionel said.

"I need to see you in my office, first thing in the morning," she said.

"What is it?" Vicki said.

"That's between Lionel and me," Mrs. Jenness said, "and his family."

Mrs. Jenness walked out the front door.

"You think she knows I'm involved with the *Underground?*" Lionel said.

"I can't think what else it would be," Vicki

said, "but what does your family have to do with it?"

"I don't have any family," Lionel said, "except you guys."

Vicki saw Rayford Steele head toward the podium. She and Lionel hurried back into the service.

Judd watched Taylor Graham closely. The pilot ran a hand through his hair and sighed. "I don't know what else to do other than tell you," he said.

"Tell me what?" Judd said.

"First of all, you kids really showed me something in Israel."

"We're not kids," Judd said.

"I didn't mean it like that," Graham said. "Gimme a break."

"I'm listening," Judd said.

"I'm not with the GC like you think," Graham said. "They gave me an order, and the best thing I could do—"

"If you're not with the GC, why are you taking orders from them?" Judd said.

"I worked for the GC just like Mr. Stahley did," Graham said. "But you don't always agree with your bosses. Mr. Stahley uncovered a lot of shady information about them. I helped him. When he died, I got even more suspicious. He had some kind of evidence that could blow the lid off Carpathia and the whole GC machine."

"And that's why you were going to deliver Ryan and me to them?" Judd said.

"Just listen," Graham said. "I can't know what the GC are doing unless I stay close. They took me in for questioning after I got back to Chicago. Now I know the time's right."

"For what?" Judd said.

"To get those secret documents out into the open," Graham said. "And to do that, I'm going to need your help."

Vicki slipped into her pew. Buck talked with Chloe and Amanda a row behind her.

"Rayford has to be exhausted up there," Buck said.

"I took him some orange juice," Amanda said. "That ought to help."

"Did you talk with Dad?" Chloe said.

"Yes," Buck said. "He really wants people to know what's about to happen so they can be ready."

"I just hope they can handle it," Chloe said. "I've seen the pages Dad's about to read. It's terrible."

"After you tricked Ryan and me, you want my help?" Judd said.

"I have to find Mrs. Stahley," Graham said.

"This is really good," Judd said. "You pretend you're our friend, you cut it real close when you took off, put on the beard and the accent to get us past those GC checkpoints, and you even rescued us and flew us out of Israel. That was fake."

"How do you know it was fake?"

"Because you flew back here to give us up! I'm not trusting you at all."

"I promise you, I didn't fake anything," Graham said.

"So those GC guys at the donut shop were for real?"

"I had no idea who they were following," Graham said. "Could've been either one of us."

"The close calls on the runway here and in Israel, those were real?" Judd said.

"Yes," Graham said. "Let me explain. When Mrs. Stahley called and asked me to help, I did it because she's family. Her friends are my friends. I wasn't happy about taking two teenagers, but you grew on me.

"When we arrived at the hotel, I got a call from GC Command. They figured out where I was and wanted me to bring you in. I went back to Haifa to get the plane and get out of there."

"You were going home without us?" Judd said.

"I figured I had to bolt and hoped you two could find a way back on a commercial flight," Graham said. "It was the safest thing to do. But they found me in Haifa, and I was forced to fly to Jerusalem. By then, you were in custody."

"This makes no sense at all," Judd said. "If you're supposed to be my friend, let me go right now!"

"I can't do that," Graham said. "You don't know what kind of danger you're in. Do you know what a double agent is?"

"Yeah, somebody who works for one government but really works for somebody else."

"That's what I am," Graham said. "I work for Carpathia and the Global Community, but I'm really working for someone else."

Judd thought a moment. He was pretty sure Graham wasn't a believer. At least he hadn't let on that he was. But if he was working for someone else, who could it be? The militia? Or was this whole conversation being taped? Maybe Graham was saying this so Judd would tell all he knew about Mrs. Stahley.

"If you're not working for the GC," Judd said, "who are you working for?"

THREE

A Frightening Future

LIONEL returned to his seat. It looked like no one had left. They all wanted to hear the next segment of Bruce's teaching, which was life-and-death stuff. Rayford Steele was reading again from Revelation 6 about those believers in Christ who would give their lives during the Tribulation. The Bible called these people martyrs.

"The Scripture says, 'I saw under the altar the souls of those who had been slain for the word of God and for the testimony which they held. And they cried with a loud voice, saying, "How long, O Lord, holy and true, until You judge and avenge our blood on those who dwell on the earth?" Then a white robe was given to each of them; and it was said to them that they should rest a little while longer, until both the number of their fellow servants and their brethren, who would be killed as they were, was completed.'

"I put Bruce in this category of one who has died for his faith," Rayford continued. "While he may not have died specifically for preaching the gospel, clearly it was his life's work and it resulted in his death."

Lionel closed his eyes. What Rayford said next gave him chills.

"I envision Bruce under the altar with the souls of those who have been killed because they believed in Jesus. He will be given a white robe and told to rest a while longer until even more martyrs are added to the total."

Lionel pictured Bruce's face, remembering the first time he had met him. Bruce was there when Lionel needed him most. Now he was waiting patiently for his white robe. Maybe he was there with Mrs. Ben-Judah and her children. *I wonder who will be the next to join them?* Lionel thought.

Rayford paused and scanned the congregation. "I must ask you today," he said, "are you prepared? Are you willing? Would you give your life for the sake of the gospel?"

As Rayford took a breath, Lionel heard a young voice cry out, "I will."

Across the balcony, Lionel spotted Ryan standing, tears streaming down his face. It was clear Rayford hadn't expected anyone to say anything out loud, but there was Ryan.

"So will I!" Lionel said as he stood. Ryan looked at him across the balcony and smiled. Three or four others in the congregation said the same. Quickly Rayford thanked those who had spoken. "I fear we may all be called upon to express our willingness to die," Rayford said. "Praise God you are willing."

Judd waited for Taylor Graham to answer. The pilot rubbed the back of his neck. Judd still didn't know if he could trust the man.

"I guess I don't know who I'm working for now," Graham said. "I was working for Mr. Stahley, but he's dead. I'm committed to keeping his wife and daughter safe. And I'm working to expose the people who killed him."

"I'm supposed to buy that?" Judd said.

"Whether you buy it or not," Graham said, "it's the truth."

Judd studied the man. Flying to Israel without knowing his loyalties had probably been a mistake. But now what?

"If all the secrets of the Global Community are down here somewhere, why aren't the GC crawling around?" Judd said. "You brought me in here like you knew they weren't going to stop you."

"They still don't know about the hangar," Graham said. "The entrance from the house is hidden. I know it's in this room, but that's all. I knew we'd be safe talking here."

"What if you're still working for the GC," Judd said, "and all this stuff about protecting Mrs. Stahley is a lie?"

Taylor Graham shook his head.

"What about the things we told you on the plane?" Judd said.

"What things?"

"The stuff about the Bible and God," Judd said. "You seemed interested."

"I am," Graham said, "but I can't say I believe it yet."

If he were really lying to me, Judd thought, *he would have told me he believed the whole thing. Maybe he's for real.*

Vicki paid close attention to the judgments and found she was finally understanding. Rayford said the scene in heaven with the martyrs could be happening that very moment.

"And if it is," Rayford said, "we need to know what the sixth seal is. Bruce felt so strongly about this judgment that he cut and pasted different translations of Revelation

6:12-17. Just remember that the Lamb in these verses refers to Jesus Christ."

As Rayford read the passage, Vicki looked at the verses in her own Bible.

" 'I looked when He opened the sixth seal, and behold, there was a great earthquake; and the sun became black as sackcloth of hair, and the moon became like blood. And the stars of heaven fell to the earth, as a fig tree drops its late figs when it is shaken by a mighty wind. Then the sky receded as a scroll when it is rolled up, and every mountain and island was moved out of its place. And the kings of the earth, the great men, the rich men, the commanders, the mighty men, every slave and every free man, hid themselves in the caves and in the rocks of the mountains, and said to the mountains and rocks, "Fall on us and hide us from the face of Him who sits on the throne and from the wrath of the Lamb! For the great day of His wrath has come, and who is able to stand?" ' "

Vicki looked up, her face white with fear. She knew that some words in Bible prophecy stood for other things, but these words seemed clear.

"I'm not a Bible teacher or a scholar," Rayford said, "but I ask you, is there anything difficult to understand about a passage that begins, 'Behold, there was a great earthquake'? Bruce has carefully charted these events. I believe the Four Horsemen of the Apocalypse are at full gallop. And I also think the fifth seal, the tribulation martyrs whose souls are under the altar, has begun."

It all fits, Vicki thought.

"Bruce's notes say more and more people will be killed because of Jesus. Antichrist will come against tribulation saints and the 144,000 witnesses springing up all over the world from the tribes of Israel.

"If Bruce is right—and he has been so far—we are close to the end of the first twenty-one months."

Vicki saw Rayford grip the podium with both hands.

"I believe in God. I believe in Christ. I believe the Bible is the Word of God. And I believe Bruce taught us well. Therefore, I am preparing to endure what this passage calls 'the wrath of the Lamb.' An earthquake is coming, and it is not symbolic."

Vicki was proud of Rayford. He had delivered the message with passion, just like Bruce. She agreed with everything he had said, but she couldn't help fear the earthquake and what might happen when it came.

Judd mulled over his next move. He could refuse to talk with Taylor Graham and see what the man did, or go ahead and trust him.

"OK," Judd finally said. "Tell me why the GC are so hot on my trail."

"There's the torching of those guys in Israel," Graham said. "But in one sense having those guys out of the way was a favor. What they really want is Mrs. Stahley."

"I don't know where she is," Judd said.

"You know more than they do," Graham said. "There was some money transferred to your bank account. They traced it back to Mrs. Stahley."

"Maybe *you* told them we were hooked up," Judd said.

"I wouldn't do that. I told you, the safety of Mrs. Stahley and Darrion are my—"

"Yeah, yeah, they're your biggest concern," Judd said.

"There's something else," Graham said. "When I got back from Indy I caught wind of something new. The top GC guys love the idea."

"What is it?" Judd said.

"Carpathia thinks he can build a world of

peace and brotherhood," Graham said. "That's why he blew up just about everything when the militia attacked."

"He wants people to get along with each other and live in peace, so he blows people up?"

"I know it sounds screwy, but it's true," Graham said. "He says the people who agree with him are going to be happy. Those who oppose him are toast."

"That means he'll wage war against people who believe what I believe," Judd said.

"And he's taking a new step toward that," Graham said. "He wants to form an organization of healthy, strong young people who are devoted to the Global Community. So devoted that they would want to make sure everybody is in line with the GC objectives."

"People ripe for brainwashing," Judd said.

"I wouldn't put it past him," Graham said.

"Would they wear uniforms, insignias, the whole thing?"

"No," Graham said. "Carpathia wants them to blend in with everyone else, but they would be trained in psychology. They would secretly inform the GC about people who oppose their views. I assume anyone who doesn't line up with the Enigma Babylon Faith would be in big trouble."

"So there goes free speech," Judd said. "What's he calling them?"

"I'm not sure," Graham said. "But he doesn't want to use the words *police* or *secret,* though that's exactly what they'll be."

"What kind of power would they have?"

"They'll carry guns," Graham said. "If they have reason to stop someone or question him or even search him, they can do it."

"Their own judge and jury," Judd said.

"Exactly. Whoever is perceived as an enemy, whoever says something negative about the Global Community, can be eliminated right there."

"Where's he going to get these people?" Judd said.

"All over the world," Graham said. "That's why I've been going along with them."

"What do you mean?"

"When they called and threatened me in Israel," Graham said, "they had no power. I could've refused and walked away. But they brought up Conrad, my brother."

"What does he have to do with it?" Judd said.

"He had nothing to do with it until they got him," Graham said. "He's in one of the camps for these new GC monitors down South somewhere. They said if I didn't help them find Mrs. Stahley, they'd put an end to his education."

"So you are cooperating with them," Judd said.

"Only to buy time," Graham said.

"How old is he?"

"About your age," Graham said. "Maybe a little younger. If I can find Mrs. Stahley and get those documents, I might be able to use them as barter. If not, I'll take them to the media and hope I can find my brother before it's too late."

Ryan could tell Rayford Steele was near the end of his message. The pilot wiped his forehead and closed his Bible.

"The seventh Seal Judgment is mysterious because Scripture is not clear what form it will take. All the Bible says is that it is apparently so dramatic that there will be silence in heaven for half an hour. We will study those judgments and talk about them as we move into that period. However, for now, I believe Bruce has left us with much to think and pray about."

Rayford stepped to the side of the pulpit, just behind Bruce's casket. He looked down and said, "We have loved this man. We have learned from this man. And now we must say good-bye. Though we know he is finally with Christ, do not hesitate to grieve and mourn. The Bible says we are not to mourn as those who have no hope, but it does not say we should not mourn at all. Grieve with all your might. But don't let it keep you from the task. What Bruce would have wanted above all else is that we stay about the business of bringing every person we can into the kingdom before it is too late."

Rayford closed in prayer. As Ryan looked up, he saw the pilot sit and lower his head. Most stayed seated, while a few quietly stood and made their way out. Ryan stayed for a few moments, then went downstairs to the meeting place.

"Why didn't they open the casket?" Ryan said.

"I think they want people to come back for a viewing later," Vicki said. "I'll be with Chaya at her mom's funeral."

Ryan looked around and saw a boy helping an old woman down the steps. As they moved toward him Ryan said, "Has anybody seen Judd?"

"I saw him, young man," the frail old woman said. "He gave up his seat for me and my . . . my daughter."

The woman took off her dark glasses and raised her silver wig.

"Mrs. Stahley!" Ryan said.

The woman put a finger to her lips and closed the door to the meeting room.

"If what you say is really true," Judd said, "I need to get back and warn my friends."

Taylor Graham looked away. "I don't think that's a good idea," he said. "With the level of risk, I'm not sure you should ever see them again."

FOUR

Chaya's Grief

RYAN hugged Darrion. She had cut her hair even shorter to look like a boy.

"Where did you guys go?" Ryan said.

"Wisconsin," Darrion said. "We have a—"

Mrs. Stahley interrupted her daughter. "We can't tell you exactly where our cottage is. It's not safe for you to know. But we had to find out if you and Judd made it back OK."

"You came all that way for us?" Ryan said.

"Taylor Graham is not our friend," Mrs. Stahley said. "He's been with us so long, I can't imagine him being disloyal to us, but now I think he's working solely for the Global Community."

"What tipped you off?" Ryan said.

"My husband's E-mail is still on the Global Community list," she said. "He received a coded message that says Taylor is cooperating. He's trying to find Judd, and in turn, trying to find me."

Vicki put her hand on Mrs. Stahley's shoulder. "Judd should be hearing this," Mrs. Stahley said. "Where is he?"

"Maybe he's back talking with Rayford or Buck," Ryan said. "I'll go get him."

"No, you stay here," Vicki said. "I'll look."

"I don't have much time," Mrs. Stahley said. "I know the GC are looking for me. I wouldn't be surprised if they were somewhere in that crowd this morning."

"But I have to get back to them," Judd said.

"If you let the others know where you are, you'll put them in as much danger as you're in," Taylor Graham said. "You can't do that. I'll get a message to them for you."

Something felt wrong. If Graham *was* working for the GC, it would make sense that he would want to find the other kids. They might lead him to Mrs. Stahley. But Graham could be telling the truth. What he said next sent a shiver down Judd's spine.

"There's also a report that your friend, Buck Williams, has Tsion Ben-Judah with him," Graham said. "Is that true?"

Rayford Steele told Vicki he hadn't seen Judd all morning. Vicki ran to the parking lot and spotted Buck and Chloe getting into their car. Before she could reach them, Buck's coworker, Verna Zee, arrived.

Vicki knew from her talks with Verna at Loretta's house that the woman did not believe in Christ. Vicki also knew that Buck was nervous about Verna and her knowledge of what he believed. She stood a few feet away and listened as Verna said, "I recognized Tsion Ben-Judah!"

"I'm sorry?" Buck said.

"He's going to be in deep trouble when the Global Community peacekeeping forces find out where he is. Don't you know he's wanted all over the world? Buck, you're in as much trouble as he is, and I'm tired of pretending I have no idea what you're up to."

"Verna, we have to go somewhere and talk about this," Buck said.

"I can't keep your secret forever, Buck," Verna said. "Do all these people believe Nicolae Carpathia is the Antichrist?"

"I can't speak for everyone," Buck said. "Verna, I took a huge risk in helping you out the other night and letting you stay at Loretta's home."

"You sure did. And you may regret it for the rest of your life."

Vicki turned and slowly walked back to the church. She heard Verna threaten Buck. If Verna told her superiors about Buck's beliefs, he could lose his job or even his life. She would talk with Chloe after the funeral and find out what happened.

If Judd was reluctant to give information about his friends, he was even more hesitant to talk about Tsion Ben-Judah. Judd knew the Global Community would stop at nothing to silence this man who had caused such a stir around the world.

"Why are you asking about him?" Judd said.

"I have to know what I'm up against," Graham said. "I don't think the GC have put you and this Williams guy together yet, but if they do, it could be bad news for everybody."

Judd silently prayed. He had acted so quickly in talking with this stranger. Now if he said the wrong thing, not only could Judd endanger his friends but the adult Trib Force as well.

"I'm not giving you any information," Judd finally said. "Maybe you're who you say you are, and maybe you're not. I'm not taking the chance."

Taylor Graham stood and walked to the other side of the room.

"Let me go, and I'll be careful," Judd said. "Or you can lock me up here, I don't care. You can kill me if—"

"I'm not going to kill you," Graham said, slamming his fist against the wall. "I'm helping you, can't you see that?" The man moved closer. "What can I tell you that'll prove I'm telling the truth?"

Judd shook his head.

"Then I'll go back and get your friends," Graham said. "And I'll bring them here one by one if that's what it takes."

Ryan noticed that Mrs. Stahley looked tired. Even though she wore heavy makeup and the wig, he could see there were big circles under her eyes.

"What are you going to do?" Ryan said.

"They'll find us sooner or later," Mrs. Stahley said. "I could try to hide, but I'm tired. And I don't like the thought of cooping Darrion up for the next few years. I have a plan."

Mrs. Stahley said she wanted Darrion to

stay with the kids. "She could live with Vicki and you, couldn't she?"

Chaya nodded. "We'd be glad to take her in," she said.

"Mother, why didn't you tell me this?" Darrion said. "What are you going to do?"

"I'm going to give myself up," Mrs. Stahley said.

"No!" Darrion shouted.

Mrs. Stahley put her hand on Darrion's shoulder. "It's the best for all of us. If I come forward peacefully, maybe I can convince them I was just concerned for you when I went into hiding."

"But you know what they'll do," Darrion said.

"Your safety means more to me than my own life," Mrs. Stahley said.

"Why do you have to choose?" Darrion said. "We can both be safe."

Mrs. Stahley shook her head. "I have to go now," she said.

"At least tell us where the secret documents are," Ryan said. "We might be able to use them to free you."

Mrs. Stahley shook her head. "I have never seen them," she said. "I only know what my husband said about them."

"And you told us they could be used to help fight the GC," Ryan said.

"I also told you they were in a secret place," Mrs. Stahley said. "I know the combination is in a file in Maxwell's upstairs office. I never asked, and he never told me where the safe was located."

"Mother, I won't let you go!"

Mrs. Stahley hugged her daughter. "Do not risk yourself for me," she said to Ryan. "Take care of my daughter."

When Vicki returned, the group brought her up to date on what had happened. Mrs. Stahley and Darrion were hugging and saying good-bye. Vicki was concerned that Judd still hadn't shown up.

Vicki made sure Darrion would be OK at Loretta's house until they returned from Chaya's mother's funeral.

"What can I expect?" Vicki said as they drove toward South Barrington.

"I expect my father to be cold," Chaya said. "He won't look at me. He'll be upset the burial has taken so long."

"Why?" Vicki said.

"Jewish custom is to bury the dead quickly," Chaya said. "Because of the bombing, he no doubt had difficulty getting her body released."

"What about the service?" Vicki said.

"You won't see anything fancy," Chaya said. "Jewish law forbids it. We are taught we are all equal in death, so the coffin is plain wood. My mother will be dressed in a simple linen shroud."

"You told me something about prayers for people who have died," Vicki said. "Will they do that?"

"You mean *shivah,*" Chaya said. "Another form of that Hebrew word means 'seven.' For seven days we mourn the person who has died. People will come and sit with the family and pay their respects. There are morning and evening prayer services at the home."

By the time they arrived at the service, Chaya had explained more about Jewish beliefs. Vicki left the flowers she had brought in the car, since Jews believe a funeral is not a time for decoration.

"I can tell this is going to be different from Bruce's funeral," Vicki said.

As Vicki and Chaya walked toward the group, a man met them. Chaya seemed to recognize him.

"I am sorry for your loss," the man said. "I have been asked to do a difficult thing."

"My father . . . ," Chaya said.

"Yes. He requested if I saw you, that I tell you it would be best for you not to be here."

Chaya looked sternly at the man. "This is my mother," she said.

"Your father says you have left the faith," the man said. "Out of respect for him and your mother, I beg you. Please go."

"Out of respect for my mother," Chaya said, "I will stay."

Instead of going to the front, Chaya and Vicki sat in the back. The rabbi recited a psalm and read a passage from the Scriptures, and the group chanted a memorial prayer.

The coffin was carried to the grave site and lowered. Chaya's father, weeping uncontrollably, took a shovel and placed some dirt on the coffin. Then people formed two lines, and the mourners passed through.

"They're saying something to your father," Vicki said.

A tear fell down Chaya's cheek. She recited the greeting, then translated it. "May God comfort you together with all the mourners of Zion and Jerusalem," she said.

Vicki noticed Chaya's father did not look at them during the entire service. When the group had left for their cars, Chaya slowly went forward to the edge of the grave. She picked up the shovel and let some dirt fall on her mother's casket. Then she pulled a small Bible from her pocket and opened it to the New Testament.

"Your mother isn't in that box," Vicki said.

"I know," Chaya said. "I believe she is with God."

She held the Bible up and read with a trembling voice, "'When this happens—when our perishable earthly bodies have been transformed into heavenly bodies that will never die—then at last the Scriptures will come true:

"'Death is swallowed up in victory.

O death, where is your victory?

O death, where is your sting?"'"

Chaya wept, and Vicki stayed with her until she was ready to return home.

Ryan inched through the line with Lionel in front of him. Hundreds of people filed past Bruce's body. The casket was open now, and on both sides of the casket were beautiful flowers.

Lionel stopped at the head of the casket, then patted Bruce's folded hands. Ryan came next. Bruce looked like he was asleep. Ryan touched Bruce's hands. They were cold and rigid.

"Good-bye, friend," Ryan managed to say, then he broke down.

Rayford Steele, who was shaking hands with people as they filed past, helped Ryan to the front pew.

"You OK?" Rayford said.

"I'm sorry," Ryan said.

"Don't ever apologize for feeling bad about things like this," Rayford said. "This is a really sad thing. Would you like a glass of water?"

Ryan wiped his eyes. "Why do people always give you water when there's something wrong?" Ryan said.

Rayford smiled. "I don't know," he said. "The other thing they do is try to make you feel better. They say things like, 'Bruce is in a better place now,' or 'Bruce is with his family.' That's true, but it's still hard to know he's gone."

"I just thought of something," Ryan said. "He's with Raymie and Mrs. Steele, too."

Rayford looked away.

"There's something I never told you, Mr. Steele," Ryan said. "Can I tell you now?"

"Go ahead," Rayford said.

"On the day of the disappearances, I came over to your house. My mom and dad weren't home, and I didn't know what to do.

I came to see Mrs. Steele or Raymie. The door was open a little, so I walked in."

Rayford listened carefully and paid no attention to the mourners who were passing by.

"I went up to Raymie's room and saw his nightclothes in a neat pile on the bed," Ryan said.

"When I found them on his bed, I folded them," Rayford said.

"Then I heard a noise down the hall," Ryan said. "You were on the floor of your bedroom, your shoulders shaking. I didn't want to disturb you, so I ran home. That's when I found out that both my mom and dad had died."

"You should've said something," Rayford said. "I could've helped."

"It still makes me sad to think about it," Ryan said. "But even though it was bad, it made me go to Raymie's church. And that's where I met Bruce."

Rayford put his hand on Ryan's neck and squeezed it. "I'm really proud of you," he said. "I wasn't around much when you and Raymie played, but I know he liked you. I can see why."

"I miss him a lot," Ryan said.

Rayford stood.

"Can I ask what you're going to do next?"

Ryan said. "Are you still going to work for the Global Community, or can you stay around here?"

"I wish I could stay," Rayford said. "But I'm still flying for the GC. I've decided I want to be obedient to God, even if that means I'm giving service to Carpathia. He wants me to be back in New Babylon next week."

FIVE
The Visitor

WHEN Vicki hadn't heard from Judd by Sunday evening, she grew more concerned. Lionel and Ryan had no idea where he might be. Chaya wanted to be alone, so she dropped Vicki off at Loretta's house.

Chloe Williams and Amanda Steele asked about Chaya.

"I guess she's doing OK, considering what she's been through today," Vicki said.

"She's facing two big losses at one time," Amanda said. "It's important for her to grieve and not shove it under the rug."

"She'll be doing fine and then, all of a sudden, she loses it," Vicki said.

"That's common," Amanda said. "It's a process. You don't grieve once and move on. Most people feel waves of bad feelings wash over them. There could be regrets or other memories that come back again and again. You realize the person is gone and is never coming back. That's really tough. Then, over time, the waves slow down and you have longer periods where you think normally. You get back into your routine."

"But it's sad that you do that," Vicki said. "For me, I lost a father. He's never coming back. But the world just goes on."

"And that's what Bruce would want you to do," Amanda said. "Think about his own story. When his wife and children were raptured, he grieved and grieved. But God used that grief. Bruce went into action and helped others come to know God."

"Is there anything I can do to help Chaya?" Vicki said.

"When I lost my mom," Chloe said, "it really helped when I chose a keepsake of hers. I gave her a necklace before I went to school, and that's one thing I still cherish."

"Maybe she can go back to her house," Amanda said, "not tonight, or even this week, but in a couple of weeks, and find something that reminds her of her mother."

"As sad as it is, I don't think her dad would allow it," Vicki said.

The talk turned to the memorial service and what had happened afterward with Verna Zee. Vicki was interested.

"Buck and I met her at the magazine office later," Chloe said. "Basically she said she knew it was Tsion Ben-Judah in that service, and I planted a little doubt in her mind."

"Did she buy it?" Vicki said.

"Not at first," Chloe said, "but then she called here, and Loretta didn't give her any information. She backed off a little, and Buck challenged her. I think she'll leave it alone for now."

"At least she came to the service like she promised," Amanda said.

"Did she mention anything about what Mr. Steele preached?" Vicki said.

"She said it was strange, all those predictions coming true," Chloe said. "When I asked her what it would take to convince her about God, she said an earthquake would be pretty hard to argue with."

Taylor Graham had been gone a long time. Judd wondered if he really would get each of the kids and bring them to the hideout, or if that was a bluff to get him to talk.

Judd sorted the facts in his mind. He wanted to believe the pilot. To have someone inside the Global Community who could give information and help him escape seemed too good to be true. Maybe it was.

Judd thought of escaping. He knew the

woods nearby well enough. He could make it to the road in ten or fifteen minutes of hard running. But something told him to stay.

Then he thought about Bruce. It was evening, and the viewing of Bruce's body was long over. Judd had missed his chance of saying good-bye to his friend.

Ryan was reading in bed when he saw Phoenix sit up. The hair on the dog's back stiffened, and he growled.

"What is it, boy?" Ryan said.

Phoenix jumped off the bed and whined. He put both paws up and scratched at the door.

"OK, show me what's out there."

Ryan followed Phoenix up the stairs. There was a light on in the kitchen, but the hallway and the living room were dark. Ryan noticed a thin strip of light under Lionel's door. Judd's door was open, and the room was dark.

Phoenix went to the front door and sniffed. He turned and barked loudly.

"What is it?" Ryan said.

As his eyes adjusted to the room, he saw the figure of a man sitting quietly in an easy chair. Ryan saw a red glow and smelled smoke in the room.

"Remember me?" the man said in a low voice.

Ryan shivered. Whoever it was had broken into the house and was waiting. Ryan did remember the voice, but he couldn't place it.

"I can't even see you, let alone remember you," Ryan said.

Phoenix was barking wildly and moved toward the man.

"Grab your dog and put him away before I do," the man said.

Ryan moved closer and grabbed Phoenix's collar.

"Put him in the closet and shut the door," the man ordered.

"I'll put him back downstairs in—"

"I said, put him in the closet," the man said, gritting his teeth.

Ryan obeyed. He felt bad putting the dog in such a small place, but he didn't have a choice.

A door opened down the hall. Lionel entered the room.

"What's all the noise?" Lionel said. "And why is Phoenix—"

"Shut up and sit down," the man said.

"We have company," Ryan said.

"How did you get in here?" Lionel said.

Ryan heard the click of a gun.

"Doesn't matter how I got in, what matters is that I'm here. Now sit down."

Lionel and Ryan sat.

"Where's your friend?" the man said.

"We have more than one," Ryan said.

"Don't get cute. The tall kid. Judd."

"We haven't seen him since this morning," Lionel said. "Why?"

"'Cause I need to talk to him," the man said.

Phoenix's muffled barks came from the closet. He scratched harder at the door, frantically trying to escape.

"You really don't remember me, do you?" the man said. He fiddled with a lamp shade and clicked on a light.

The flash nearly blinded Ryan. The man had turned the lamp away from himself and onto the boys. Ryan shielded his face with his hand, and the shadowy sight of the man sparked his memory. The long black coat. Short hair. Under the L tracks. The man with the gun.

"Remember me now?" the man laughed.

"He's with the Global Community," Ryan said to Lionel. "He was going to kill Judd and Vicki and Mr. Stahley."

"Until this little runt jumped me," the man said.

"What do you want with Judd?" Ryan said.

"It's personal," the man said. "We're looking for a few missing people. That Stahley woman and her kid. A pilot named Graham. You know where any of them are?"

"For a professional bad guy, you have a hard time keeping track of people," Ryan said.

Lionel flinched. "Cool it," he whispered to Ryan. "I think I know how we can get out—"

"Knock it off," the man yelled.

Lionel sat up.

"Maybe I need to show you I mean business." The man raised his gun at Lionel, then pointed it a few inches to the right. "This will quiet the little pooch," the man said.

"No!" Ryan screamed.

Ryan heard a quick spurt from the silencer and a thwack behind him as the bullet went through the hollow door and into the closet. Phoenix stopped barking. Ryan turned to see the huge bullet hole. The hole was at the same height as the doorknob.

"Stay where you are," the man said, "unless you'd like one of these for yourself."

"You better not have hurt my dog!" Ryan said.

Phoenix whimpered inside the closet and barked again.

"Listen to him," the man said. "Your dog's fine. But I'll aim a little lower next time unless you tell me where your friend is."

"We don't know," Lionel said. "He was supposed to meet us after a funeral today, but he didn't show up."

"Not good enough," the man said, raising his gun again.

"It's the truth!" Ryan screamed, standing to block the door.

"Sit down!"

"No!" Ryan said.

"I told you, get out of the way—"

Ryan heard a loud bang and closed his eyes. Then he heard another spurt from the gun. Glass shattered. Ryan opened his eyes and saw the man running for the front door. He opened it, held his gun in front of his face, then pivoted into a shooting stance. When he didn't see his target, he shouted at the boys to stay where they were. Then he was gone.

"What happened?" Ryan said.

"Get Phoenix and let's get outta here," Lionel said. "I'll explain on our way to Vicki's place."

Lionel collapsed on the couch when he arrived at Vicki's house. Ryan fell to his knees, gasping for air, as Phoenix bounded through the door. Vicki got Phoenix a bowl of water and waited for Lionel and Ryan to catch their breath.

"What happened?" Vicki said when they could finally talk.

"First," Lionel said, "I don't think they followed us, but in case they did, who's here?"

"Darrion, Chaya, and me," Vicki said. "What's going on? Did you find Judd?"

"No," Lionel said, "but we did find out we're not the only ones looking for him."

Ryan explained who the man with the gun was and what had happened. "I still don't know why the guy took off like that," he said.

"You didn't see him?" Lionel said.

"Who?" Ryan said.

"Just before I whispered for you to cool it," Lionel said, "I saw a guy look in the window."

"Another GC guy?" Vicki said.

"I don't know who he was," Lionel said, "but he got a good look at Ryan and me. He moved around to the front to get a look at the other guy. I figured they weren't together. That's when you stood up."

"I wasn't about to let him blow Phoenix away," Ryan said.

"He shot at the window, and the other guy

took off," Lionel said. "That's when we bolted."

"What did the guy at the window look like?" Vicki said.

"It was pretty dark, but I could tell he was tall," Lionel said. "Looked like a swimmer."

Ryan asked a few more questions and then shouted, "It was Taylor Graham!"

"What would he be doing at the house?" Vicki said.

"Looking for Judd," Ryan said, "or me. Whatever the reason, I'm glad he showed up."

"I feel like the walls are closing in," Lionel said. "Let's get Darrion and Chaya and get outta here."

"Wait," Vicki said. "First, I'm not going anywhere until we find Judd. Second, if we run, they'll think we're guilty of something, and we're not! If you miss the meeting with Mrs. Jenness tomorrow, people from the school could be looking for you as well."

"If they find us here, they'll find Darrion," Lionel said. "That'll connect us with Mrs. Stahley, who's wanted for murder!"

"And we all know it was the GC who killed Mr. Stahley," Vicki said. "We have to keep our lives as normal as possible until we find Judd and figure out what to do."

Judd looked for a way to escape from his underground prison, but he found none. Taylor Graham had locked him in a room deep inside the hangar. The heavy metal door was impossible to open, so Judd spent his time looking through the desk and the bookshelves that lined one wall of the room.

In the center drawer of the desk Judd found paperclips and stationery. In the back he discovered a shoe box filled with old baseball cards. *These have to be worth a fortune,* Judd thought. Mixed in was what looked like a key card to a garage. Judd tossed the box back into the desk and kept looking.

In the bottom drawer Judd found huge pages rolled into a scroll. He cleared the desk and unrolled it, looking at the precise drawings.

A blueprint, Judd thought. As he studied it closer, he realized it was a drawing of the Stahley home and underground hangar.

There has to be a passage from the house to here, Judd thought.

He found drawings for the upstairs, the kitchen and patio area, the basement, and then he found an arrow with the word "entrance" scrawled underneath.

Judd flipped the page over and saw a drawing of the underground hangar. He found another arrow drawn in a small room in the back of the hangar. When he studied it further, he realized he was in that very room.

Now we're getting somewhere, Judd thought. *If I can get into the house, I'm free. But how?*

The arrow on the drawing pointed to what looked like the bookshelf. Judd pulled books away, hoping a panel would move. He took each book off the shelf and put it back, but nothing happened.

Next he tried moving the actual shelves, but they were somehow anchored to the wall. Mr. Stahley had placed decorative plates and mugs along the shelves. Behind one was a square, silver plate with a slot in the middle. A red light flashed above the slot. He studied it for a moment, then quickly went back to the desk and retrieved the weird card in the shoe box.

It fit perfectly, but when he inserted it, nothing happened. When Judd pulled the card out, however, a green light flashed below the slot. Something was moving behind Judd. A door? A vault?

Judd turned and was amazed to see a section of the tile floor rising. Underneath, a safe with an electronic combination came into view.

SIX

Lionel's Dilemma

THE NEXT morning Lionel retrieved some clothes from Judd's house and headed for school. Vicki said she would be praying for him and stood across the hall from the principal's office while Lionel went in.

The school secretary was just getting in and asked him to wait. Finally, she buzzed Mrs. Jenness.

The principal opened the door and ushered Lionel in. Inside, a burly, black man about the size of Lionel's father stood and embraced him.

"I don't mean to scare you," the man said. "I've just heard so much about you, I feel like I know you."

"Who are you?" Lionel said.

"This is Mr. Sebring," Mrs. Jenness said. "He called me last Friday about meeting you."

"Nathan Sebring," the man said, "but my friends call me Nate. Your mother called me that when we were kids."

"My mother?" Lionel said.

"Lucinda was one of my dearest friends," Nathan said. "I called her Cindy. I knew your father as well. Fine man."

Mrs. Jenness asked them to sit. "We had trouble locating you with your current address," she said. "The house was empty. Boarded up, actually."

Lionel didn't speak. He didn't want to talk about where he was staying until he was asked.

"I knew your mama when we were little kids," Nathan said. "Some of your family's still down South and when I asked about you, they said—"

"I didn't think I had any family left down South," Lionel said. "Didn't they get taken in the disappearances?"

"Sure, some of 'em did," Nathan said, "but a couple were left. I think they heard through your Uncle André that you were still alive. I'm sorry to hear about his passin'."

The two stared at Lionel as if he was supposed to know what to say. Lionel stood. "Well, it was really nice meeting you," he said. "I'd better get to class."

"Now hold on a minute," Nathan said, taking Lionel's arm. Lionel looked at the man's hand, and he took it away. "Your family asked me to come for you," Nathan continued. "They gave me papers."

"They're in order," Mrs. Jenness said.

"I told them I'd come and get you. They made me promise not to come back unless I brought you back."

Lionel forced a smile. "That's very kind of you," he said, "but I don't know the family back there anymore. I wouldn't feel comfortable."

Nathan looked at Mrs. Jenness. "He'll get used to it in time," Nathan said. "He'll be like a bird let out of a cage down there."

"Lionel," Mrs. Jenness said, "if it's true that you have no family here and there are relatives who want you to live with them, I don't see that you have any real choice in the matter."

"Now you've got that right, ma'am," Nathan said. "The boy just doesn't understand how much love those people have for him." Nathan looked at Lionel. "If you knew how much they cared, you wouldn't put up a fuss."

"I don't want to go," Lionel said. "I'm happy where I am."

Nathan cocked his head. "Now if that don't beat all," he said. "I'm sorry. I guess I just don't understand the culture up here. A man rides hundreds of miles on a train to find somebody he's never met, and when he finds him . . . mm mm mm."

"You could have phoned," Lionel said.

"I did phone the only place that has contact with you," Nathan said. "And Mrs. Jenness, who has been a wonderful help, offered her complete assistance."

"Lionel," Mrs. Jenness said, "you have a right not to go, but Mr. Sebring and the family also have the right to petition the Global Community Social Services."

"And I'll do it, too," Nathan said. "Out of respect for your relations down South, of course."

"Can he really do that?" Lionel said.

"I can and I will," Nathan said.

Lionel felt alone. Bruce was dead. Judd had disappeared. He was glad Vicki was outside waiting for him.

"Can you give me some time to think it over?" Lionel said.

"You can have the whole day," Nathan said. "I scheduled train tickets leaving tomorrow for the two of us. Where can I come talk to you?"

"Why don't you leave me your hotel number?" Lionel said. "I'll call you this evening."

Judd had slept fitfully on a cot Taylor Graham left outside the door. Judd dragged it inside and heard the door lock.

"Hey, don't I get something to eat?" Judd had yelled, but Graham didn't respond.

Judd awoke the next morning and heard moaning in the next room. He banged on the door and yelled. In a few minutes, Graham returned with orange juice and sweet rolls, but the man winced when he put the food on the desk.

"What's wrong?" Judd said. Then he noticed the bloodstain on the back of Graham's shirt.

"Had a little trouble at your house last night," Graham said.

"*My* house?" Judd said.

"I told you I was going to bring your friends here one by one," Graham said. "But I was a little late. The GC had a guy talking with Ryan and another kid."

"Right." Judd smirked. "You're just saying that to—"

"I'm telling the truth," Graham said sternly. "The guy saw me and fired. It only grazed my shoulder, but it hurts like crazy."

"I've gotta get outta here," Judd said. "Do you know what happened to my friends?"

"Don't have a clue," Graham said. "But I'm not letting you go."

Judd stood and ran past the pilot. Graham stuck out his foot and held it tightly against the door. Judd turned and lunged at Graham, who easily stepped aside. Judd went sprawling on the floor.

"Whether you believe it or not," Graham said, "I'm doing this for your own good."

Vicki called an emergency meeting of the Young Trib Force that afternoon. The kids ordered pizza, but everyone was so upset, no one felt like eating.

"I can't believe it," Ryan said. "Why do they come for Lionel now, after all this time?"

"Don't ask me," Lionel said. "Seems like I'd have some kind of say in it. I don't even know these people."

"What about your friend at the GC Social Services," Chaya said to Vicki. "Couldn't she help?"

"I called Candace from the school this morning," Vicki said. "She told me she'd do everything she could, but it doesn't look good. If the guy really is empowered by the family, Lionel could fight it, but he'd eventually have to go."

"And if that's true, I'd only be making them mad if I draw this thing out," Lionel said. He put his head on the table. "I don't know what to do."

"Maybe you should go with Judd," Ryan said, "wherever he is."

"Don't joke about it, OK?" Lionel shouted.

"What'd I do?" Ryan said.

"This is my life we're talking about," Lionel said. "They're taking me away. Do you understand that?"

Ryan got up and slammed his chair into the table. "I hope you do go," Ryan said. "The sooner the better."

Ryan ran out of the room. Chaya stood, but Vicki motioned for her to stay. "Let him go," Vicki said.

The kids sat in awkward silence. Finally, Lionel said, "I wish Judd were here."

Vicki did too, but she didn't say it. Judd had been their anchor. Whether he made the right decision or not, he took charge. The kids could lean on him. Even though she wasn't the oldest, she felt a responsibility to take his place.

"Judd's not here," Vicki said, "and neither is Bruce. We've been saying all along we want to make our own decisions and that God can lead us just as well as he can lead older people."

Lionel looked at Chaya. "Please tell me there's something in the Bible that'll let me stay," he said.

"The closest thing I can come up with is the verse about obeying authorities," Chaya said. "I know it's not what you want to hear."

The group threw around ideas and options. Lionel could go into hiding. He could stay and fight the system. Or he could go with Nathan. After a few minutes Chaya took the floor.

"No matter what you decide," Chaya said, "there are some things in Bruce's notes we need to talk about. He made it no secret that we would one day become the mortal enemies of the Antichrist. We've done a lot of worrying about money, but one day, even to buy a loaf of bread, you'll have to take a mark on your forehead or your hand."

"Wait a minute," Lionel said. "What do you mean? Like a stamp or something?"

"It's not clear what form it'll take," Chaya said, "but if you don't have it, you'll be in trouble. We won't be able to fake it. And once you take the mark, you've chosen sides with the devil. You're lost forever."

"What if you don't take it?" Vicki said. "Is there any hope for those people?"

"The people who don't have the mark will have to live in hiding," Chaya continued. "Their lives won't be worth anything to the Global Community, so they'll have to take care of themselves."

"I don't like the sound of that," Lionel said.

"Bruce wrote about this, and I think Dr. Ben-Judah agrees," Chaya said. "Cash is going to be meaningless soon. We need to take what money we have left and convert it to gold."

"What I have left wouldn't buy an ounce," Lionel said.

"Why gold?" Vicki said.

"Cash might be phased out pretty soon," Chaya said. "Gold can still be used for food and supplies. That is, until the day comes when we're forced to choose whether to take the mark of the Beast."

"Then we have to put that in an edition of the *Underground*," Vicki said. "Especially this thing about taking the mark."

"I agree," Lionel said. "Buck Williams is coming out with a *Global Community Weekly* article that spells out the great earthquake that's coming. You could use some of his material, too."

"What do you mean *I* should?" Vicki said. "You're not going to be part of it?"

"I've made up my mind," Lionel said. "It tears me up to say this, but I'm going to call the guy and tell him I'll go."

Judd was angry. He didn't know why he was being held. If the Global Community wanted to question him, they could have done it at any time. But here he was, alone, separated from his friends.

"Let's say I believe you," Judd said. "Let's say you are keeping me here for my own good. What happens then?"

"We work together," Taylor said. "We find Mrs. Stahley and Darrion and figure out where those documents are."

"Can you get a message to my friends?" Judd said.

"I can send an E-mail right now," Graham said.

Graham plugged in an incredibly light-weight computer and turned it on. A window opened with a video display of news. Graham was about to open his E-mail program when Judd stopped him.

"Look at that," Judd said.

On the screen was a news anchorwoman with a graphic of Maxwell Stahley behind her. Graham turned up the audio as the anchor introduced a reporter.

"We're live at police headquarters," the reporter said, "where only moments ago a dramatic arrest was made in the Maxwell Stahley murder case."

Judd was horrified to see video footage of Mrs. Stahley being led away from a hotel parking lot.

"She was dressed as an old woman," the reporter continued, "but someone at the hotel recognized her from news reports, and police took Louise Stahley into custody."

The video footage ended, and the reporter was shown outside police headquarters. "Authorities tell us the woman will remain here overnight, then she'll be handed over to the Global Community early tomorrow morning."

Taylor Graham cursed and slammed his hand against the desk. "There goes our chance to find those documents," he said.

Judd stood and took the key card from his pocket. He knew Graham was telling the truth now. He slid the key card into the slot, and the safe rose from beneath the floor.

"I know where the documents are," Judd said. "Now all we have to do is figure out the combination."

Lionel put his suitcase down in the foyer of Bruce's house. It was late. No one seemed to want to look at him. Lionel shook hands with some and hugged others. Vicki was in tears.

"Do you know where he is?" Lionel said.

"Bruce's room," Vicki managed.

Lionel found Ryan staring out Bruce's window.

"I'm sorry for snapping at you," Lionel said.

"Yeah, it's OK," Ryan said flatly. "I didn't mean what I said either."

"I don't hold it against you," Lionel said. "We're all pretty raw right now."

"So you're giving up?" Ryan said.

Lionel frowned. He didn't want to get into it with Ryan again. If things had to end, he wanted them to end well.

"I don't think you're rid of me yet," Lionel said. "A couple of years and I'll be on my own."

"A couple of years is a long time when there's only five left altogether," Ryan said.

"I don't know why this has happened," Lionel said. "I keep thinking maybe there's somebody down South who needs to hear the truth. My going might be the only way they'll hear it."

Ryan turned. "I'm sorry . . . about everything," he said.

"We had some good fights," Lionel said.

Ryan smiled.

Lionel saw a van pull into the driveway. Nathan Sebring got out.

Lionel shook hands with Ryan.

"Call me," Ryan said.

"You bet," Lionel said.

As Lionel grabbed his suitcase, Darrion came out of her room, crying. "They've arrested my mother," she said. The others came to comfort her.

As he got in the car, Lionel looked back at the house. The kids were standing outside. He had been through so much with these friends. He allowed a thought to cross his mind: *This might be the last time I see any of them in this life.*

SEVEN

Judd's New Friend

JUDD looked at his E-mail early the next morning, but there were no answers from Vicki, Lionel, or Ryan. Taylor Graham had showed Judd how to send and receive mail without tipping the GC. "It's unsafe to use the satellite phone," Graham had said.

Judd tried to think of who else he could reach to get to the kids. He sent a message to Buck, Chloe, and even Dr. Ben-Judah. While he was on-line, the computer blipped.

"Incoming message," a voice said.

The screen switched, and Judd saw words being typed by Dr. Tsion Ben-Judah. "Judd, I have had no contact with your friends, but I must ask you a question," the rabbi typed.

"Go ahead," Judd typed back to him.

"I am receiving hundreds of responses already to postings on the Internet," Dr. Ben-Judah said. "As you can imagine, I am unable to respond to them all. A few are from younger readers. I would like to send a note of thanks and tell them a colleague will respond to their questions or concerns. Would you assist me with this important task?"

A colleague with Tsion Ben-Judah? Judd thought. Judd certainly had the time now that he was also in hiding.

"I would be honored," Judd wrote. "Send the messages immediately."

Vicki was glad Ryan didn't argue about staying at Judd's house. When a neighbor approached them and asked about a strange man snooping about, Vicki told Ryan to get back in the car. Ryan slept on the couch at Vicki's place and was ready for school early the next morning.

Vicki checked her E-mail before she left and let out a yelp when she opened the message from Judd. Ryan read over her shoulder.

"Vicki," Judd wrote, "I'm safe and staying with a friend. Ryan knows him, too. He's convinced I'm in real danger. Ryan knows this place—it's behind a 'green hillside that opens up.' I've made a discovery but need more information to help D's mother. Let me know when you get this." The note was signed "JT."

"What does he mean?" Vicki said. "Is he in Israel?"

"The only green hillside I can think of is the one that leads to the underground hangar at the Stahleys," Ryan said.

"You think his discovery is the secret documents?" Vicki said.

"That's something that could help Darrion's mother," Ryan said. "Write him back and tell him the combination is in Mr. Stahley's office upstairs."

Judd read Vicki's message carefully. Vicki told him Lionel was gone. Judd was stunned.

When Taylor Graham returned later that morning, Judd asked if they should bring Ryan into hiding with him.

"Not yet," Graham said. "I went to your house last night but couldn't find him. From the reports I get, he's safe. Which is more than I can say for myself."

"What are you hearing?" Judd said.

"I picked up a radio transmission a few minutes ago," Graham said. "They have GC posted in the house. They've found out about the documents, but they don't know where they are. We have to get that combination."

Judd showed him Vicki's message. "The combination is inside the house," Judd said. "Do you know how to get inside?"

"Max never told me how he came and went from the house," Graham said. "I always used the outside entrance."

"Can't we just use some kind of explosive on it?" Judd said.

"Material's too strong," Graham said. "Plus we'd draw attention to ourselves with a blast that big."

"What are you going to do?" Judd said.

"I'll have to try and sneak in from the outside," Graham said.

A knock on the hotel room door awakened Lionel. He stretched and felt something crawling on his arm. Nathan Sebring had chosen a shabby hotel near downtown Chicago. During the drive Lionel could tell the man didn't want to talk. He wouldn't explain where they were headed or what time their train left the next day.

Nathan answered the door and welcomed an overweight man he called Tom.

"Good work, Chuck," Tom said to Nathan. "They bought the accent?"

"I told you not to worry," Nathan said.

The two exchanged papers, and Tom handed Nathan a wad of cash.

"This is your next assignment," Tom said.

Nathan looked at Lionel. "Change of plans, big boy," Nathan said. "You're getting a ride from my friend."

"I thought we were going on a train," Lionel said. "And why is he calling you Chuck?"

Nathan grabbed his overnight bag and laughed. "Nice meetin' ya," he said. Then he was out the door.

"What about my family?" Lionel said.

Tom told Lionel to get dressed.

"I need to take a shower, bugs are crawling all ov—"

"I said, get your clothes on and get in the van!" Tom yelled.

Vicki was in a daze at school. The loss of Lionel made her feel more alone. Mrs. Jenness called an all-school assembly, and Vicki found her friend Shelly sitting near the back.

"You're not gonna believe this," Shelly said. "I was working in the office yesterday when the Global Community called. This is mandatory."

"They made the school call this assembly?" Vicki said.

"It's a grief awareness seminar," Shelly said.

Mrs. Jenness introduced the speaker as a

therapist. She also attended an Enigma Babyon One World Faith congregation and had personally met Nicolae Carpathia.

"Two good reasons to get up and walk out," Shelly whispered.

The speaker began by asking how many people had lost family members and friends in the last two years. Almost every hand went up.

"You have the power within yourself to overcome anything," the woman said. "No matter how bad your situation, if you learn to trust yourself and your feelings, you can become the person the Global Community needs."

Judd had free reign of the hangar. For exercise, he jogged. Graham showed him a stash of food that could last months if they needed it. Judd and Graham tried in vain to find the passageway from the hangar to the house.

"I'm headed topside," Graham said. "I'm gonna chance it. Wish me luck or whatever you do."

Judd turned to the computer. He spent most of his time there, communicating with his friends and those who e-mailed Tsion. Some of the kids who wrote the rabbi wanted more evidence, but most of them had come to Christ and were asking what they should do with their faith.

One message stood out. The screen name was "Pavel." The boy wrote Tsion and said he wanted to understand the truth about the man named Jesus. Tsion suggested that Judd send him a copy of the Scriptures and excerpt some of Bruce's teachings. Judd did that, but he also struck up a conversation. Judd asked where Pavel lived and what his family had been through during the war.

"We have not experienced any harm during the war," Pavel wrote. "My father works for the Global Community here in New Babylon. One day he mentioned the potentate was upset by the message of the rabbi in Israel and of the men who preach at the Wailing Wall. I became curious. I read the rabbi's messages and listened to the men at the Wailing Wall."

Judd couldn't believe it. The son of someone at Global Community headquarters was interested in the gospel!

Judd explained the life of Christ as clearly as he could. "Jesus was born of a virgin and remained sinless his entire life. He was not just a good man, he was perfect. He was God in the flesh. Sin separates a person from God forever, and every person on earth has sinned. But Jesus' death paid the penalty for anyone who believes in him. If a person asks for God's forgiveness, God answers and freely gives salvation."

Judd included Scripture references and a personal message at the end. "If you have video capabilities and other questions," he wrote, "tell me when it would be safe and we'll talk."

As he wrote the message, Judd wondered if this boy was actually who he said he was. For all Judd knew, "Pavel" could be Nicolae Carpathia himself.

Judd said a prayer and pushed the Send button. *I don't care who it is or what his motives are,* he thought. *Everybody needs to hear this before it's too late.*

Vicki couldn't wait until it was time for questions. Two microphones were positioned in the front and back of the auditorium. At each end, students lined up and waited their turn. Vicki was second in line at the microphone in the back.

Kids who had lost family members in the bombings were in tears. Most of the kids were energized by what the therapist said.

They were into the positive message. Vicki's heart went out to them. What the speaker had said made her angry.

"I can tell you loved your brother very much," the woman said to a freshman at the front of the room. "And I can tell you where he is right now. You have him right in your heart. You have to keep your brother alive. And you have to trust yourself to do that."

Vicki rolled her eyes. She was up next.

Judd's video hookup with Pavel was successful. The kid looked small and wore thick glasses. He had blond hair and sat low in his chair, so he stayed in the bottom of the picture while he spoke. Pavel could understand six languages, but he could speak only four. He apologized for his English.

"I cannot tell you who my father is," Pavel said, "but it is true. I am in the apartment building in Nicolae Carpathia's compound."

"You know that Dr. Ben-Judah's message is not very popular with the potentate," Judd said.

"I understand," Pavel said. "But since the disappearances and the war, I have been searching for answers. The ones the Global Community gives do not satisfy."

Judd's computer blipped. "Hang on, Pavel, I need to check something," Judd said.

The message looked weird. He could tell from the message window that it wasn't from any of his friends. He gasped when he saw it was from the Global Community. It read: "Global Community Priority Directive: The pilot is in custody. Continue the search for the daughter and the two boys. Search their homes and schools first."

The speaker pointed to Vicki and smiled. "You have a question?" she said.

"Yes," Vicki said. "If you knew for sure where a person was after they had died, wouldn't that be the best hope of all?"

The woman looked bewildered. "I don't understand the question," she said.

Mrs. Jenness stood and moved toward the woman.

Vicki continued. "Let's say your father dies on the day of the bombings and you're really bummed," she said. "But you know without any doubt that your dad went to heaven. Wouldn't that help in your grief?"

Mrs. Jenness whispered something to the woman, and she nodded. "Heaven is a state of mind, not a real place," the woman said.

"I think we should leave matters of faith to our religious leaders. Next?"

"No, answer the question!" Vicki said.

"You, in front?" the woman said.

The girl at the next microphone looked back at Vicki. It was Shelly!

"I'd like to hear you answer her question," Shelly said.

Someone in the crowd yelled, "Answer it!" Vicki heard a few boos and some applause. Things were quickly getting out of hand.

"All right," the woman said, trying to regain control. "If a person knew what happened after a loved one had died, in a psychological sense that would give him or her hope. But we have to deal with reality here. And the reality is, we can't know what's beyond this life until we've gone there."

"That's where you're wrong," Vicki said. "We *can* know."

"So you're saying you can judge whether a person is good enough to go to heaven?" the woman said.

"Yeah, who made you God?" someone said.

"I can tell you that *nobody* is good enough to go to heaven," Vicki said. "Every one of us has sinned. But God made a way for us—"

"That's enough," Mrs. Jenness said. Global

Community guards moved toward Vicki.
"Byrne," the principal shouted, "sit down or you'll be escorted out of here."

Vicki stepped away from the microphone. Everyone turned to look at her. She didn't want to betray her faith, but she also didn't want to give Mrs. Jenness any more ammunition against her.

She sat. During the rest of the meeting, three girls passed notes to her asking to talk with her when the assembly was over.

Judd gave Pavel some new materials and asked if he could get in touch with him later in the day. Pavel said he could safely talk at midnight Judd's time.

As soon as the line was free, Judd contacted Tsion Ben-Judah. He had to find some way of protecting Ryan and Darrion.

Lionel was hustled into the van by another man. Several other boys were already inside. They all looked scared. A cage separated the driver and the backseats. Lionel felt like he was going to prison.

"Where are they taking us?" Lionel asked

an older boy in the seat in front of him. The boy didn't respond.

Lionel watched the traffic from inside the tinted windows of the van. They went south on the expressway until the road forked. One sign said Memphis, another said Indianapolis. The driver stayed to the right and drove toward Memphis.

Ryan was playing dodgeball in gym class. He was one of three remaining players when the teacher blew his whistle. "Daley!" he yelled. "Get over here."

"I wasn't hit, Coach, really," Ryan said.

"Get over here."

The coach was a long-faced, thin man who acted tough. But Ryan knew he was fair.

"Somebody wants to see you in the office," the man said.

"Can I finish the game?" Ryan said.

The coach smiled. "You go on, it looks pretty important."

Ryan ran out of the gym and up the stairs to the long hallway that led to the office. He felt weird wearing his gym uniform in this part of the school. He looked out the big window by the office and stopped. Pulling into the parking lot was a white car that said,

"Global Community Security." Two men got out and walked toward the school. Ryan didn't know the one on the left. The one on the right wore a long, black coat and had short hair.

"This doesn't look good," Ryan muttered. He turned to head back to the gym for his clothes. Before he took a step, someone grabbed his arm.

EIGHT

In Hiding

VICKI met with the three girls at lunch after the assembly.

"You really showed that Global Community lady," one girl said.

"I only stood up because I don't think she was telling us the truth," Vicki said. Vicki briefly told her story. The other girls listened while they ate. When she was almost finished, Shelly tapped Vicki's shoulder and nodded toward the entrance.

Mrs. Jenness scanned the room with a scowl.

The three girls picked up their lunch trays and moved away.

Ryan felt the viselike grip on his arm and heard a man whisper, "Move down the hall and don't look back."

When they were nearly to the gymnasium, Ryan glanced up. "Buck!" he said.

Buck Williams hustled Ryan out the back entrance. "My car is still around front," Buck said.

"I just saw GC Security pull in," Ryan said.

"They're after you," Buck said. "Dr. Ben-Judah reached me at the office. Judd heard they were coming to get you."

"How would he know that?" Ryan said.

"We can find out later," Buck said. "Right now I need to get the car and get you somewhere safe."

Ryan hid in the parking lot and watched the school carefully. He could see the gym entrance through a window. The vice-principal and two GC goons were talking to his teacher.

Ryan hopped in the backseat when Buck arrived. Someone was hunkered down on the floor.

"I guess this is Buck's witness protection program," Darrion said.

"What did you say in the office?" Ryan asked Buck.

"I told them I was with the Global Community, flashed my credentials, and asked to see you," Buck said. "They took one look at my clearance card and didn't ask questions."

"Where are we going?" Ryan said.

"We have to get you to safety," Buck said. "The GC have both Mrs. Stahley and Taylor Graham in custody."

Ryan gave a low whistle. "We must have been wrong about Graham," he said.

As they drove, Ryan asked Buck questions about the adult Tribulation Force. Rayford Steele was preparing to return to New Babylon. Amanda, his wife, was staying to help Chloe with the materials Bruce left behind. Tsion Ben-Judah was in hiding, though Buck didn't say where, and Buck was working on a *Global Community Weekly* article.

"What's it about?" Ryan said.

"I'm taking Bruce's message and turning it into a cover story," Buck said. "I've assigned reporters from offices in several countries to interview different religious leaders. I'll include their answers in my article."

"What are the questions?" Darrion said.

"Just one," Buck said. "Will we suffer the 'wrath of the Lamb'?"

"Wow," Ryan said. "Has anybody been assigned to talk with that Enigma Babylon guy?"

"Peter Mathews?" Buck said. "I did that myself. He thinks the book of Revelation is just literature. He says the earthquake is symbolic and that if God exists at all, he or she is a spirit or an idea."

"Sounds like what I used to believe," Darrion said.

Buck pulled up to a stoplight in Mount Prospect. "The only question is, where do I take you?" Buck said.

Ryan smiled. He knew a place where no one would find them.

Vicki sat through the geology lecture, wondering if she would get another chance to talk with the girls she met in the assembly. She was thinking of the *Underground* and what the next issue would contain when she heard her teacher say something about an earthquake.

"I have a friend who attended a funeral the other day," the teacher said, "where someone brought up the idea of a worldwide earthquake." The teacher laughed, and several students snickered as well.

"People who buy into religion put their minds on the shelf," the teacher continued. "There has never been nor will there ever be a global earthquake."

The teacher drew a diagram on the chalkboard. "We've talked about this before.

Earthquakes are caused by faults. These underground plates rub against each other. But tell me, if this one smacks against this one, do you think there will be an earthquake over here?"

"No," the class responded.

"Of course not," the teacher said. "It's not logical. If you believe there's going to be a worldwide earthquake, you probably believe in a global flood and that a man and his three sons saved all the animals in a boat."

While the others laughed, Vicki took notes.

Lionel sat in the dark van, his stomach growling. He hadn't eaten since the night before. When the driver stopped for gas, he yelled, "Nobody talks!" Both the driver and the other man got out.

Lionel knocked on the window and asked, "When are we gonna get something to eat?"

The driver stuck his head in the door and cursed. "I said nobody talks!" he screamed.

"Better keep your mouth shut," a boy behind Lionel whispered when the man was gone. "He'll probably give us something before too long."

Lionel introduced himself.

"I'm Jake," the other boy said.

"Where are you from?" Lionel asked.

"Detroit. They got me yesterday."

"Where's he taking us?" Lionel said.

"Someplace down South," Jake said. "We don't know for sure, but somebody heard the guy mention Alabama."

Lionel shook his head. "They told me there were family members looking for me," he said. "I thought the man who took me was a friend of my mom's."

"That happened to a couple others in here," Jake said. "They grabbed me right off the street."

"Your family will come for you, won't they?" Lionel said.

"Don't have family," Jake said.

Lionel felt sorry for him but didn't know what to say. "What could they possibly want with us?" Lionel said.

The large boy in front of Lionel turned. "They'll have to give us a bathroom break before long," he said. "We're jumping them when they do. Got it?"

Lionel nodded as the driver and Tom got back in the van. The driver pulled over to the side of the road, opened a cooler, and passed bottles of water to the boys. Lionel thought it was the best thing he had ever tasted.

Ryan asked Buck to drive to the church. Buck's eyes widened when Ryan opened the secret entrance to the Bible hideout. "Bruce had this built at the same time . . . as the other construction."

"I got you," Buck said.

Ryan knew Dr. Tsion Ben-Judah was probably only a few yards away in his underground shelter, but he didn't dare bring up the subject. He didn't want to endanger the rabbi or Darrion by revealing it. Still, he wished he could sit and talk with the man. It seemed clear to Ryan that the rabbi was destined to preach the gospel to thousands in the next few years.

Buck ran out for fast food and brought it back. Ryan and Darrion ate hungrily as they planned their next move.

"I think I should stay here," Ryan said. "Can you find a place for Darrion that's safe?"

"We can use Loretta's apartment," Buck said.

"I don't want to hide," Darrion said. "I want to help my mother."

"Hang tight," Ryan said. "We'll do our best."

Judd was on-line at midnight. Through the video link, Pavel said he did not go to a conventional school but had teachers come to him.

"I am alone for another hour," Pavel said. "But I need to tell you something."

"What is it?" Judd said.

"Here," Pavel said. He reached toward the camera and positioned it lower. Judd saw a wheelchair.

"You may not want to talk to me any longer," Pavel said, "but I feel you should know the truth."

"You're in a wheelchair," Judd said. "Big whoop."

"What did you say?" Pavel said.

"I said it's not a big deal," Judd said. "It doesn't make a difference to me."

"It makes a big difference to most people I know," Pavel said. "I cannot do what others do. When some find out, they no longer want to be my friend."

"Their loss," Judd said. "You're smart, you ask questions, you think things through. You may never win the one hundred-yard dash, but there are more important things in life."

Pavel beamed. "You sound like my mother," he said.

"Your mother's a sharp lady," Judd said.

"Was," Pavel said. "She vanished."

Judd felt a chill go down his spine. "Pavel, do you know why she disappeared?"

"I do not know," Pavel said. "She never complained, but I thought it might be because taking care of me was so difficult."

"I'm sure that wasn't it," Judd said. "Did your mother ever read the Bible?"

"My father would not allow it," Pavel said. "He says religion is for those who are weak, and I do not want to be weaker than I already am."

The boy paused and reached beneath his desk. "I found this on my mother's bed the morning of the disappearances," Pavel said. He held up a small black book.

Judd told Pavel why his mother had disappeared. Jesus Christ had come back for true believers. His mother had to be one of them.

"She tried to talk with me about God, but I wouldn't allow her to," Pavel said. "My father can be a very stern man."

"Don't wait any longer," Judd said. "You can be sure right now that you're a true follower of Jesus."

"How?"

"You've read the material I sent," Judd said. "Do you believe what those verses said?"

"Yes," Pavel said.

"You know you can't work your way to God or do enough good things to get you into heaven, right?"

"Before now I didn't even believe in heaven," Pavel said, "but yes, I do believe."

"If you know you've sinned, you can pray right now and ask for forgiveness." Judd outlined a prayer and then watched as Pavel bowed his head.

"God, I am sorry for what I have done," the boy said quietly, "and I have done so many bad things. I believe you sent your Son, Jesus, to die for me. And I believe he did rise from the dead. Please forgive me. Amen."

Pavel looked up. "Was that all right?" he said.

"That was great," Judd said.

"Does that mean when I die I will see my mother again?" he said.

"It sure does," Judd said.

Lionel awoke, his head bobbing up and down with the bouncing of the van. He saw the exit for Tupelo, Mississippi. Then the van pulled into a rest area.

"You boys have two minutes each," the driver said. "We'll take you in groups of three." The man held up a gun and shoved in a cartridge. "In case you get any ideas, we both have one of these."

As the men exited, the boy in front of Lionel turned. "This is it," he said. "Whoever is with me helps me jump these guys, all right?"

The kids around Lionel nodded. Lionel stiffened. He didn't mind giving his life for a good cause, but this one seemed stupid.

"Why don't we just see where they're taking us first," Lionel said.

The bigger boy turned and held up a fist. "I hope you're not in my group," the boy said, "but if you are and you don't help, I'll get you."

"I'm just saying we might be making a mistake—"

"You'll make a mistake if you don't help," the boy said.

The first group went into the rest area with the driver and quickly returned. The man named Tom herded the next three—Lionel, Jake, and the bigger boy. He sneered at Lionel. "Better do what you're told," the boy said.

The driver was a wiry-looking man with a stubbly beard and bad teeth. He mumbled for them to go to their right, sticking the end of the gun deep into his coat pocket and waving it.

The lobby was empty. There were slots with maps and brochures of vacation destinations. Pictures of Elvis Presley dotted the walls. Lionel went into the bathroom first, followed by Jake. The last boy stumbled, dropped something on the floor, then knelt in the open doorway.

"Giddup," the man with the gun said.

"Can't without some help," the boy said.

"Wait!" Lionel shouted from inside the bathroom.

But it was too late. As the man looked up, the boy on the floor punched him hard in the stomach. The man wheezed and fell backward. The boy jumped to his feet, pulled the bathroom door closed, and locked it.

"Couldn't get his gun," the boy shouted. "Open that window!"

Jake was on it. "It's stuck," he said.

Lionel heard coughing and sputtering outside, then a shout from the man at the van.

"Don't do this," Lionel said.

"Too late now," the boy said. "You're in this as much as me."

The boy yanked at the window. The second time, the window broke from its hinges, leaving a small opening. "You first," the big kid said to Lionel.

"No way," Lionel said.

"Suit yourself," the boy said.

Jake went out, then the bigger boy. Lionel heard footsteps, then gunfire. If he stayed, he might get hit.

Lionel hopped up to the opening and fell to the ground in some bushes. He easily caught up with the other two as they crossed a creek.

In the distance Lionel heard the door break and more shots. He was glad to be alive, but he had no idea what trouble he was in.

NINE

Discoveries

JUDD was anxious to leave the hangar and be with his friends, but he couldn't leave without the secret documents. They were the only hope for Mrs. Stahley and Taylor Graham. As the hours passed, his hope faded.

He spent most of the day on the computer, answering questions and sending material. Every chance he got, he moved around the room looking for the entrance to the house.

He was at the computer when he heard a noise. Voices. People moving around. Knocks on the wall.

Judd sat still. He could hear himself breathe.

"It sounds hollow here," a man said on the other side of the wall.

"It sounds hollow in a lot of places," another said. "Keep looking."

When the men moved on, Judd let out a sigh of relief. He had to have a plan of escape in case the GC discovered the entrance to the hangar.

Lionel and the other two boys ran through the night. When they came to a swampy area, Lionel warned them of snakes. "They have water moccasins down here," he said.

"They're not out this time of year," Jake said. "Are they?"

The boys went around the swamp and came upon an abandoned farmhouse. Lionel couldn't see inside and didn't want to chance going in. With no flashlight or matches, they huddled on the porch and waited for light.

Something moved inside.

"Probably a raccoon," the big boy whispered. "Maybe a possum."

A bat flew through the window, and the boys heard an earsplitting screech. "I'll take my chances with the snakes," Jake said, as all three fled the house.

Lionel said very little as he and Jake followed the bigger boy. By morning they were tired and hungry. Lionel was covered with burrs from head to foot.

"You think they'll get the police on us?" Jake asked the big boy.

I hope they do, Lionel thought. *Then I can tell them what really happened.*

"They won't chance using the cops," the big boy said. "What they're doing is illegal." The boy looked at the sunrise. "I have a good feeling. If we've made it till now, we're probably all right."

The boys followed a dirt road that eventually led them to a small general store. Lionel had enough change for one bottle of soda. They were sharing the drink when Lionel saw the van. Jake and the other boy ran. Lionel just stood by the store and waited.

Vicki assigned the articles for the *Underground* and worked late into the night on each one. Judd had done an excellent job providing material from Dr. Ben-Judah. Chaya was editing Bruce's sermon notes from the memorial service. Mark had written about the "wrath of the Lamb" prophecy and what damage a worldwide quake would do.

She hoped to add these to Buck Williams's material and an article about taking the mark. If it all came through, it would be the most convincing newspaper the kids had ever published.

Vicki talked with Buck after reading an

advance copy of his *Global Community Weekly* article. "As you can see," Buck said, "I've tried to take an objective viewpoint."

"But there's enough truth in here for people to figure it out," Vicki said. "How does this kind of reporting compare with the other things you've done?"

"I've done Man of the Year stories, covered famous personalities, breaking news events," Buck said, "but I've enjoyed this more than all the others combined."

"You have everybody in here," Vicki said. "Nicolae Carpathia, faith guides from around the world . . ."

"But the scoop of the year is getting Tsion Ben-Judah," Buck said.

"How are you going to explain getting an interview with him to your bosses?" Vicki said.

"Simple." Buck smiled. "Dr. Ben-Judah learned about the story over the Internet and submitted his view from a secret location."

Vicki could see the excitement in Buck's eyes. Within a week, millions of people would read what she held in her hands.

"My hope is that people will get far enough into the article to see what a converted Jew from Norway says about the earthquake," Buck said.

Vicki flipped to the next-to-last page.

"No one should assume there will be shelter," the man was quoted as saying. "If you believe, as I do, that Jesus Christ is the only hope for salvation, you should repent of your sins and receive him before the threat of death visits you."

As much as he liked the Bible room, Ryan hated being cooped up. Buck was able to find an old laptop computer for him, but since there was no telephone in the room, Ryan had no connection for E-mail. He knew he shouldn't bother the rabbi.

Bruce had equipped the room with a cable hookup, so Ryan kept up with the news. News stations ran footage of the arrest of Mrs. Stahley and Taylor Graham, but nothing more was said. They were being held in connection with the murder of Mr. Stahley.

Each day Ryan was supplied with food by Chloe or Amanda. Ryan loved his visits with Amanda because she reminded him of his mother. Chief in his mind was Darrion's safety.

"You don't need to worry about her," Amanda said. "We have a visitor coming next week, so we asked Sandy Moore if she could stay with her."

"Is that the computer guy's wife?" Ryan asked.

"Right," Amanda said. "At first, Sandy said she didn't know if it would work. Then she talked with Donny, and he said he had the perfect place."

"Good," Ryan said. "The GC would have no reason to look there."

Amanda asked how Ryan felt about being alone.

"I'm OK," Ryan said. "I just want to get out of here as fast as I can."

"I'm counting the days until I see Rayford again, too," Amanda said. "He's in New Babylon. I enjoy the work Chloe and I are doing, but I'd give anything for us to be together."

"Must be tough," Ryan said.

Amanda Steele pulled a chair close to Ryan. "I'm not sure anything can be as tough as what you're going through," she said. "You've lost everything you've ever known. Your parents. Your best friend, Raymie."

"But I've gained a lot, too," Ryan said. "That's what Bruce said when I talked about his family. He said it was worth losing everything just to make sure he was right with God."

"Bruce was right," Amanda said. "If he were here, he'd tell you how proud he is of you."

Lionel had been placed in the locked van while the two men caught Jake and the other boy. The men had given up the search the night before and delivered the other kids. Then they returned.

"We knew we'd catch you kids someplace where there was food," the guard with the bad teeth said.

"You're gonna pay for gettin' away," the other said.

They crossed the Mississippi state line into Alabama and finally reached the compound. Several older teens roughly led the three into a small, dingy building. Lionel was locked in a single room with no light.

He awoke to the sound of birds. It was morning. Lionel imagined the nest of little ones breaking through their eggs, waiting for their mother to bring food. *What freedom,* he thought.

It had been two days since he had eaten a full meal. Lionel could tell he was getting weaker. He had always said he was "starving to death" when he was the least bit hungry. Now he felt like he really was.

Ryan finally got up the nerve to knock on Tsion Ben-Judah's door. He was sure the rabbi was being hidden there. He just didn't know if the man could hear his knock.

"Dr. Rabbi, sir," Ryan called, "it's me. Ryan. I don't want to disturb you. I know you're doing important stuff and all."

Ryan sat down by the concrete blocks. If the door was as thick as it looked, the rabbi wouldn't be able to hear a sledgehammer.

Suddenly the door opened, and a ray of light hit Ryan full in the face. "Dr. Ben-Judah, sir," Ryan stammered.

"Come in, Ryan," Tsion said.

"I know I'm not supposed to come down here, and I'm awfully—"

"It is all right," Tsion said.

"But Mr. Williams and the others will be upset—"

"Don't worry," Tsion said. "I will tell them I needed the company."

Ryan looked around the enclosure. It was sectioned into three rooms. There was a full bath and shower, a bedroom with four double bunk beds, and a larger room with a small kitchen on one side and a living room/study on the other.

Ryan went straight to the computer. While

Tsion was talking, a message came from Judd. He told the rabbi about the voices on the other side of the wall.

"Can I?" Ryan said.

"Be my guest," Tsion said.

Ryan typed, "Hey, Judd, hang in there. The troops are coming."

"Who is this?" Judd typed.

"Your pal, Ryan. Could you go outside and climb into a window upstairs?"

"The information I have is that the house is surrounded," Judd said. "I'm hoping to find the entrance, then sneak up there at night."

Ryan signed off and thanked the rabbi. "I won't come down here anymore," Ryan said.

"You were no bother," Tsion said. "I will pray that you are able to make it out soon."

"I'm sure I will," Ryan said.

On Friday afternoon, Lionel was released from the building and given food. He tried not to eat too fast, but he ate and drank all that was given to him in less than a minute.

Lionel was led to a meeting hall, where all the kids sat on the floor and listened to a man talk about the Global Community.

"You came here as boys, but you'll leave as men," the man said. "Our hope is that you'll become an asset to the brotherhood of mankind."

Lionel saw Jake in the corner. They met after the meeting.

"Did you get any of what the guy was saying?" Lionel said.

Jake shook his head. "My stomach's still too empty to listen," he said. "But I do know one thing. Every one of us means more money to the guys running the place."

"What do you mean?" Lionel said.

"They've got some racket going with the Global Community," Jake said. "For every kid that comes here, they get X amount of dollars of support from the GC."

"Even if they get here the way you and I did?" Lionel said.

"The GC doesn't know that," Jake said. "And there's something else. They're training us for something. I don't know what, but one guy said when we leave, we get to carry a gun."

"How'd you find that out?" Lionel said.

Jake pointed to someone sitting in the corner. "That kid over there," he said. "His name's Conrad."

Ryan slipped into the church office. The front doors were locked, and Loretta had gone home. Ryan dialed the number and gave his address. He went out the back of the church and stayed in the shadows. Night was falling, but he wanted to use the rest of the daylight for his trip.

When the cab pulled up in front, Ryan looked both ways, then ran. When he got in, the cabbie said, "You the only one?"

"Yes, sir," Ryan said.

"Let me see your money," the cabbie said.

Ryan held out a few wadded bills and some loose change. "I counted it," he said. "There's twelve dollars and about $1.37 in change." Ryan handed the man the address. "You think it's enough?"

When they arrived, the cabbie shut off the meter. "That's $10.50," he said.

Ryan looked at his money. "I don't know how to do tips," he said.

The cabbie rolled his eyes. "If I do a lousy job, don't tip at all. If I drive carefully and show my wonderful personality, you could give me 20 percent."

"How much is that?" Ryan said.

"I don't know," the cabbie said. "Just give me the $10.50 and we'll call it square."

Ryan handed him the whole thing. "Keep the change," Ryan said. Before he shut the door, he looked back. "I've always wanted to say that."

Late Friday night, Judd sent the final draft of his article for the *Underground.* Talking with Vicki via E-mail was fun, but it wasn't the same as being face-to-face. He admired her for the way she had kept going. That she was preparing another newspaper for the people at school showed she cared. She could have played it safe. Not Vicki.

Judd wondered whether his life would ever be "normal" again. Would he be able to go out in public? After questioning Taylor Graham and Mrs. Stahley, would the GC turn to him for answers?

He was tapping his fingers against the computer keyboard when he heard a strange thump come from the hangar. He turned off the light and moved toward the door. The hangar was pitch black.

"Anybody there?" Judd said in a loud whisper.

Nothing.

"Oh, well," Judd said out loud. He turned, then heard it again. It was coming from the door.

Heart racing. Thinking of a way out. *If it's GC, what do I do? Surrender? No way.*

Judd heard a creak, then felt something against his skin. Night air. The smell was wonderful. Fresh. Then Judd realized someone had found the mechanical box near the woods. They had probably seen the door open by now. Judd stood back. Armed guards would descend any moment. How could he escape?

Judd had located two motorcycles in the hangar while jogging. One was smaller, and from the size of the helmet, he guessed it was Darrion's. The other was a large dirt bike. He hadn't tried to start it for fear it would alert the GC team on the other side of the wall. Now it didn't matter. They knew.

Judd ran to the motorcycle. He strapped on the helmet, then looked for the ignition key. It wasn't there. *On the wall inside the study!* Judd thought.

There wasn't time to retrieve the key and start the machine, so Judd rushed to the door and hit the button to close it. In the moonlight he saw a figure running toward him.

Come on, door!

Judd rushed for the key, grabbed it, and turned. Before the door closed, the figure somersaulted into the room.

"Ryan!" Judd exclaimed. "What are you doing here?"

Ryan smiled and cocked his head. "I came to help," he said. "You going somewhere?"

Judd took off his helmet and shook his head. "You could have been shot!" he said. "You might have led them right to me."

"I didn't," Ryan said. "But you were right about them being around the house. There have been three out there all evening."

"How long have you been here?" Judd said.

"Long enough to know we'd better find that entrance," Ryan said.

TEN
Secret Documents

JUDD and Ryan searched the room again, taking out every book and every drawer. Nothing. Early Sunday morning, Ryan suggested they have some kind of church service.

"Let's get Tsion in on it too," Judd said.

Tsion joined them by computer. Judd felt weird singing with just two other people. They sang softly so they wouldn't be detected. Tsion asked Ryan to read a passage from Luke.

Ryan read, "'As they were walking along someone said to Jesus, "I will follow you no matter where you go." But Jesus replied, "Foxes have dens to live in, and birds have nests, but I, the Son of Man, have no home of my own, not even a place to lay my head."'"

"There is a great cost to following Jesus,"

Tsion said. "Those who were his disciples did not realize it at the time, and I confess I am like them. And you are as well. We had no idea what would happen, and where God would take us. But here we are. God be praised."

Tsion talked further of being willing to go and do whatever God wanted. Judd and Ryan prayed for wisdom and courage for the days ahead.

As Judd prayed, he opened his eyes and looked up. He noticed a panel in one corner of the ceiling he hadn't seen before. When they had said good-bye to Tsion, he got a chair and looked at it more closely.

"What's up?" Ryan said.

"I think we may have been looking in the wrong place," Judd said. "I thought the entrance in here would be through the wall, but maybe it's up here somewhere."

Judd poked and pushed at the three-foot square, but nothing happened. When he moved the chair he saw another square on the floor the same size and in the same spot as the one above.

"I don't get it," Ryan said. "Is the entrance up there or down here?"

Judd sat back and scratched his head. "Maybe it's nothing," he said.

Ryan took a run and jumped on the square

in the floor. Ryan's feet came down hard. Judd heard a noise. The panel above moved to the side to reveal a hole. At the same time, the panel Ryan was standing on raised off the floor.

"Hurry and get on," Ryan said.

Lionel tried to figure out why the men would have taken him. He received the answer from Conrad.

"They have a lot of ways to get kids," Conrad said. "They snatch some off the street. Some they go after for a reason."

"Like you?" Lionel said.

"My older brother is in the GC," Conrad said. "My hunch is they brought me here to punish him for something."

"What about me?" Lionel said. "A guy came to my school. He had papers."

"Somebody had to have tipped them," Conrad said. "I know they have shady connections to people in prison. Does anybody in jail know you?"

"LeRoy and Cornelius!" Lionel said. "Of course."

"Who are they?"

"Two guys we helped the cops put in jail," Lionel said. "They killed my uncle. Either one of them could have given my name out of revenge."

"It doesn't matter how you got here," Conrad said. "The question is, what're you gonna do about it?"

Lionel shook his head. "These guys are gettin' in my head," he said. "They make us exercise until we drop, then only give us a little food. Then they say the same things over and over again. And most of the guys are falling for it."

"Most of the guys don't know the truth about the GC," Conrad said.

Lionel sat up. "And you do?" he said.

Vicki rode with Chaya to the service at New Hope Village Church. A week after the service for Bruce, the pews were packed. Vicki thought Bruce would be pleased. On the way home, Vicki talked with Chaya about Amanda's suggestion.

"I don't think my father would allow me inside the house," Chaya said.

"You can call him and try," Vicki said.

"Maybe I'll call the rabbi and ask him to help," Chaya said. "Perhaps the grief over my mother has softened my father's heart."

The panel lifted until Judd and Ryan were through the ceiling. A ladder was fastened to the wall and led up.

"Let's see where it goes," Ryan said.

"Not now," Judd said. "We'll wait until late tonight."

Lionel listened as Conrad talked about his brother. "He flies for the GC," Conrad said, "but he told me he doesn't trust them."

"Why does he still work for them?" Lionel said.

"He's loyal to his boss, not the whole GC," Conrad said. "When they grabbed me, I heard them tell my brother not to do anything stupid."

"What are they trying to do to us?" Lionel said.

"I can't figure it out," Conrad said. "I know they want us to be part of the Global Community in some way, but it's not clear. They're definitely using mind control on us."

"Mind control?"

"The way they make us parrot stuff back to them," Conrad said. "They say things over and over. In the small groups it's almost like some of the guys are in a trance."

"They're not gonna control me," Lionel said.

"How can you fight it?" Conrad said.

"I was hoping you'd ask," Lionel said.

Judd tried to sleep during the day, but he and Ryan were too excited. They heard very little movement on the other side of the walls, but they didn't want to take any chances.

Late that night, Judd and Ryan activated the entrance and climbed the ladder into the secret passageway. When they got to the top of the ladder, they stepped onto a small landing in front of a huge panel. Judd turned on his flashlight and noticed a blinking sensor on the wall. There was no slot for a key, so Judd put his hand over it.

A latch clicked. The panel moved slightly open. Judd nodded, and Ryan pushed the panel slowly. Ryan and Judd stepped through the opening. They were now inside the plush Stahley house.

On the other side of the panel was a painting of the Stahley family. "Don't close it all the way," Judd whispered. "We might not be able to open it again."

The two stood still and listened. No movement in the house. Judd saw that they were on the main floor of the house, and they would need to go up a flight to find Mr. Stahley's office.

They took a step, then realized their tennis shoes squeaked on the tile. They took off their shoes and placed them gently by a pillar that held an antique vase.

When they reached the stairwell, Judd saw movement through the windows. He held up a hand, and Ryan stopped. A GC guard with a gun was moving back and forth on the patio.

On the second floor they tried three rooms before they found Mr. Stahley's office. If they turned on a light or even used the flashlight, Judd knew the GC might notice. Pictures and papers were strewn about the floor. Judd found the desk, then groped in the dark for the filing cabinet.

It was locked!

"Try opening the middle drawer," Ryan said. "Sometimes that releases the others."

Judd opened the middle drawer, then tried the other. It opened!

Judd patted Ryan's head.

Judd grabbed half the stack of files and moved away from the desk. Ryan followed his lead and took the other half. They slipped down the hall to the bathroom. Laying the files in the tub, Judd drew the shower curtain, placed his hand over the flashlight, and turned it on. A reddish glow provided enough light to see.

"You flip through them while I hold the light," Judd said.

The files looked like any homeowner's. There were folders for investments, bills, warranties, and taxes. Mr. Stahley was organized.

Ryan flipped through them and shrugged. "What would it be under, Secret Safe Combination?"

"What did Mrs. Stahley say about the combination?" Judd said.

"Just that it was in a file in Mr. Stahley's study," Ryan said.

Judd flipped to a file titled "Construction." Inside he found bills and contracts for the house. There was nothing listed about the underground hangar. Next he looked in the warranties. There were receipts for a home theater, several cars and motorcycles, and household appliances. In the back was a small receipt from The Stockholm Safe Company.

Judd scanned the writing but found no unusual set of numbers. "This has to be it," he said.

"Look on the back," Ryan said.

Judd turned the paper over. On the

bottom corner of the page was a string of numbers. Judd stuffed the paper in his pocket and turned off the flashlight.

Judd and Ryan stopped when they heard a door open and close downstairs. Voices. Two men.

Judd's stomach tightened. His heart beat faster. If the men noticed the open picture, they were sunk. A light went on. Judd and Ryan moved into the shadows.

"What's this?" a man said. "I didn't see those here before."

"Somebody's here!" the other man said. He keyed his walkie-talkie and ordered other guards inside. "You search upstairs, I'll go downstairs."

Judd and Ryan watched as a guard ran up the stairs. The man's gun was equipped with a laser. He looked both ways at the top of the landing. Judd and Ryan were to the right. The man ran left, down the hall. It would only be a few moments before he discovered the files in the bathtub.

Judd and Ryan quickly moved down the stairs. The front door opened, so Judd waved Ryan through the kitchen. Two more guards were in the house.

"Where do you want us to search?" the

man said into the microphone attached to his shoulder.

"Main floor and the kitchen," came the reply.

Judd and Ryan stole to the other entrance to the kitchen. If the guards came this way, they were dead. If they came the other way, Judd and Ryan still had a chance.

Judd saw two pinpoints of red light behind them and moved into the living room. He and Vicki had first met Mr. and Mrs. Stahley in this very room. They kept moving, quickly but quietly. They passed the stairs and heard the guard yell, "I've found something! There's stuff in the bathroom."

Now they ran full speed toward the opening in the wall. Judd wasn't about to worry about his shoes at this point. He wanted to get into the wall and latch it shut before the guards saw them.

Judd made it to the opening first and opened the picture. Ryan stumbled around the corner and fell headlong into the antique vase. It shattered on the floor with an incredible crash.

"Hurry up!" Judd said.

The men converged on the two boys. Ryan tried to stand, but he kept slipping on the waxy floor. In the darkness, he looked like

Phoenix on Judd's kitchen floor when Ryan brought out a treat.

Ryan finally made it through the hole and started down the ladder. Judd closed the picture just as the red lights converged on their end of the hallway.

"Where'd he go?" a man said.

Judd trembled as he descended the ladder. He slid the last ten feet to the ground. Ryan jumped on the square, and the two were led back into their hideout.

Judd was shaking as he pulled the combination to the safe from his pocket. He fumbled for the key card but couldn't find it.

"Wait," Ryan said. "I had it last." Ryan opened the desk drawer and rummaged through it.

"Hurry up!" Judd yelled.

From the other side of the wall, Judd heard a man yell, "They're down here somewhere, I can hear them!"

Ryan found the card and shoved it in the slot. The safe rose, and Judd began punching in numbers. When he hit the last one, the door to the safe popped open with a *whoosh.*

Inside were a stash of bills, some gold coins, and a folder. Judd grabbed the folder and flipped it open.

"Evidence against the Global Community

and Nicolae Carpathia," was written at the top of the page. What followed was a point-by-point listing of facts uncovered by Mr. Stahley after the death of his brother.

"Bring it right here," the man on the other side of the wall yelled.

"We have to go," Ryan said.

"Hang on," Judd said as he glanced at the document.

Judd heard some kind of saw grinding through the wall.

"How thick is that wall?" Ryan said.

"Not thick enough," Judd said, folding the document and stuffing it into his pocket. Ryan followed Judd into the hangar. Judd locked the door behind them. "That'll hold them for a few more minutes."

Judd showed Ryan the motorcycles. They threw the helmets away, grabbed the keys, and pumped the starters. Ryan's bike fired up immediately. Judd's sputtered and coughed but started on the third try.

"If we get separated," Judd said, "we meet at the church."

"Got it," Ryan said.

Judd punched the button to the outside door. As it slowly opened, Judd saw a rotating blade cut its way through the door behind them.

Judd took the lead down the hill. There

was no headlight on the bike, which made driving dangerous. Judd looked back and saw one man talking into his microphone.

Judd was nearly to the Stahleys' driveway when a vehicle shot out of the bushes and cut him off. Judd turned and followed Ryan, the GC vehicle not far behind. Ryan pointed to the woods on the other side of the property.

While Judd and Ryan rode along the side of the hill, the GC vehicle couldn't. It went into the valley and up the other side. By that time, Judd and Ryan had neared the woods and had a lead. If they reached the trees, the GC would have to backtrack to the access road.

Judd's body rattled on the motorcycle. He turned once more to see the pursuers. Then he lost control of the bike.

Ryan looked back just as Judd's front tire hit a rock. The bike upended and sent Judd sprawling. Ryan braked hard, turned around, and raced back.

Judd was sitting up when he got there. "Go!" Judd yelled.

"I'm not leaving you," Ryan said.

"I'm hurt," Judd said. "I can't ride. They're almost here. Now go!"

Ryan felt awful leaving his friend. When he made it to the woods, he looked back long enough to see that the GC vehicle had over-taken Judd.

The documents, Ryan thought.

But it was too late. Ryan gunned the bike and sped through the trees toward Vicki's house.

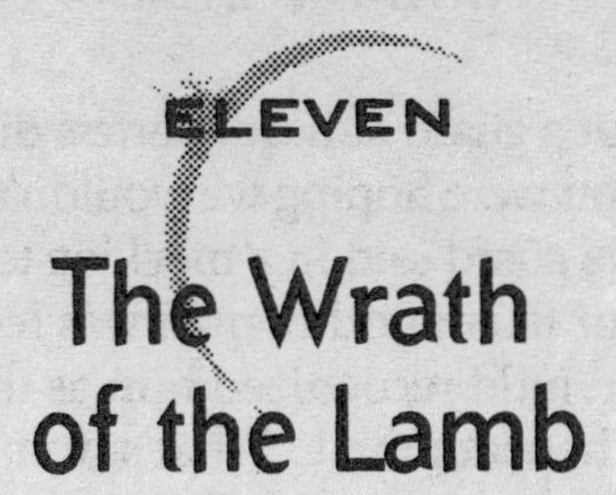

ELEVEN

The Wrath of the Lamb

VICKI could hardly believe Ryan's story when he arrived at her house early Monday morning. With the documents in the hands of the GC, she knew they had little hope of helping Mrs. Stahley, Taylor Graham, or even Judd.

Ryan nodded. Phoenix huddled close and licked his hand.

Judd was sore and dazed as he sat in the Global Community headquarters. Though he hadn't broken any bones in the fall, he had strained his neck and shoulder. The GC guards hadn't helped any with the way they had arrested him.

Judd prayed they wouldn't find the documents, but a guard at headquarters discovered them. "You were hoping we wouldn't find these," the guard said in a mocking tone.

An hour later another man was led into the room. Judd recognized him as the gunman beneath the L. "That's him," the short-haired man said. "Where's the other kid?"

"We don't know, sir," another guard answered.

"I'm talking to him," the man said.

"I'm not telling you anything," Judd said.

"Better think hard," the man said. "You've got a record." The man ticked off a list of Judd's violations and said, "You're a prime candidate for reeducation. I wouldn't be surprised to see you shipped out of here by next week."

Lionel decided his best plan of action was to obey his captors until he could find a way back home. If they thought he was one of them, he could escape. He hoped to do so with his new friend, Conrad. Lionel had told Conrad his story, but the boy seemed skeptical. Lionel backed off and prayed for him.

The group quickly tapped Lionel for leadership. By the middle of his first week in camp, he knew the GC slogans and chants by heart. He was drawn into the inner circle, where they explained their mission.

"You are part of an elite group of young people," a GC official told them. "You have been chosen to be the eyes and ears of the Global Community and our leader, Nicolae Carpathia."

Yeah, right, Lionel thought.

On Friday evening, Vicki called a meeting to pray for Judd and give an update. They had heard nothing from Judd since his arrest.

"I'm taking the *Underground* to school Monday morning," Vicki said. "I want to thank you all for your help and ask you to pray for me."

Chaya said she wouldn't be able to drive Vicki, so Mark offered.

"Where are you going?" Vicki asked Chaya.

"My father has allowed me one hour Monday morning to go through some of my mother's things," she said.

The kids prayed for her, then Lionel. Ryan asked about Darrion. She was still with Donny Moore and his wife. The discussion turned to Ryan's safety.

"The GC may not care about you," Vicki said. "With Judd, Taylor, and Mrs. Stahley in custody, they might leave you alone. But I'm not taking any chances."

"I haven't gone outside the whole week," Ryan said.

"I know," Vicki said, "but I want you to promise me in front of everybody. You won't go outside, right?"

"I promise," Ryan said.

Monday morning Mark helped Vicki load a duffel bag full of copies of the *Underground* into his car.

"I hear security is as tight as ever," Mark said. "How are you going to get it inside?"

Vicki held up a key. "Shelly gave me this yesterday morning," she said. "I had a copy made and got it back before they knew it was missing."

"What's it for?" Mark said.

"The gymnasium," Vicki said. "I'm putting the *Underground* in the gym lockers."

Vicki thanked Mark and lugged the duffel bag to the gymnasium entrance. The key fit perfectly. She locked the door and walked across the basketball courts. Her footsteps echoed in the building. She put the bag down and looked down both halls. Empty.

She started with the boys' locker room. She placed several copies of the paper in each locker, then closed the door. Where she found a lock, she stuffed the pages through the vents in front. She hoped the first-period class would take one, then leave the rest for others.

She was nearly finished when she sensed someone watching her. She turned. No one was in the room. She saw a movement in the coach's office. She picked up the bag and headed for the door. She opened it and found Mrs. Jenness staring at her.

"Byrne," she said. "I saw someone walk through the gym on the monitors."

The cameras! Vicki thought.

Vicki backed up. Mrs. Jenness grabbed the duffel bag and pulled out a copy of the *Underground*. She looked startled. "You!" she said. "It *was* you."

Mrs. Jenness rifled through the lockers, stuffing the papers back in the bag. She marched Vicki to the office and ordered a Global Community guard to collect the papers from the rest of the lockers.

"You're staying right here," Mrs. Jenness said as she sat Vicki in her office. "This time I have evidence, and I'm not letting you out of my sight!"

For a whole week the Global Community tried to uncover more information from Judd, but he kept silent. Finally they led him to a holding cell for transport. Judd hadn't received treatment for his injuries, but he felt better. Now he was anxious to see where they were taking him. He was definitely going to a reeducation camp, but he had no idea how severe the treatment would be. The camps ranged from a minimum Level 1 camp to a maximum Level 5.

The door opened, and three other prisoners were led in. Judd gasped when he realized one of them was Taylor Graham. The man looked sick. He was bruised about the face, and he walked with a limp.

"Taylor, it's me, Judd."

The pilot's left eye was swollen shut, so he turned his head to see Judd. He smiled. "So they finally found you?"

Judd explained what had happened. When he told Graham about the secret documents, the man winced. "I wish we could have saved those," Graham said. "The GC probably destroyed them, so there's no hope for Mrs. Stahley and me."

"Where is she?" Judd said.

Taylor Graham shook his head. "They told

me she was sent out of here late last week," he said.

Several armed guards led them to the transport area. "You two, get over here," one guard said to Judd and the pilot. "You're going to Level 5."

Vicki sat in the office and watched Mrs. Jenness read the *Underground.* The woman sneered as she read. When she was finished, Mrs. Jenness bundled the copies and ordered them burned.

After school was under way, Mrs. Jenness made two phone calls. "No, I do not want someone to pick her up," she said. "I'll bring her in myself."

Vicki glanced at the clock as they left the school. It was 9:00 A.M.

Chaya found her mother's clothes piled in bags for a nearby homeless shelter. She picked up a sweater and smelled her mother's perfume. In her mother's room, she found pictures and jewelry. Chaya remembered how she used to play with her mother's box of treasures.

Chaya located the family photo albums and pored through them. She wept and laughed as she remembered vacations and graduations and the way her mother was always there.

Chaya couldn't decide which memento to take—a golden broach she had given her mother or an empty photo locket.

The door downstairs opened and closed. She looked at the clock. It was 9:18 A.M.

Judd Thompson, Prisoner #4634-227, was handcuffed and sitting by Taylor Graham in the third seat of the Security Transport vehicle. The STV drove west of Chicago, then south along Interstate 55.

"How many Level 5 places are there?" Judd said.

"There are two in Illinois," Taylor Graham said. "One is close to the Wisconsin border near Rockford. The other is close to a little town named Streator, about two hours south."

Judd watched as the scenery changed from apartment buildings and storefronts to cornfields and farmland. They exited I-55 and headed west. Judd noticed an unusual amount of dead animals on the road. Skunks, raccoons, and deer littered the two-lane road.

They passed a farmhouse and a huge grain silo. The weather vane on top swayed.

Vicki watched Mrs. Jenness drive with determination. The principal had her revenge now and was going to enjoy every minute. Mrs. Jenness's knuckles turned white as she gripped the steering wheel.

"I told you I'd get you, Byrne," Mrs. Jenness said.

"Didn't anything in the *Underground* or in the service for Pastor Barnes get to you?" Vicki said.

"If you want to believe that stuff, it's your business," Mrs. Jenness said. "But you'll never come in my school and shove it down our throats again."

Vicki looked away. The electric lines and light poles seemed to be moving, but there was no wind.

Ryan was watching television in the basement when Phoenix bounded into the room.

"Hey, boy, you glad to see me?" Ryan said.

Phoenix barked and put his paws up. Then he ran in circles around the room.

"Looks like you need to go out," Ryan said. "Sorry I can't go with you."

Phoenix raced Ryan up the stairs and jumped on the front door.

"No, you gotta go out back," Ryan said. Ryan opened the screen door and Phoenix bolted from the house, yipping and barking like Ryan had never seen before.

"That dog's goin' crazy," Ryan muttered.

Lionel was in the exercise yard of the compound when someone yelled, "Snake!"

Boys ran to the edge of the yard, then retreated to a nearby porch. Lionel watched as snakes crawled out of their holes and raced across the compound. There had to be at least a hundred of them, all slithering and hissing.

Lionel saw squirrels in a nearby tree skitter to the top, then jump to the limbs of another tree. A huge cloud of birds darkened the sky, then they were gone.

Then Lionel felt it.

The ground.

Shaking.

He looked for a place to run. To hide. Then he remembered. There was no such place.

Chaya met her father downstairs by the piles of clothes.

"I am sorry," she said. "I got caught up with all the pictures and I forgot—"

"We agreed you would be gone by now," Mr. Stein said. "I don't want to talk with you."

"Please, Father," Chaya said.

A fine mist fell around Chaya. Then a chunk of plaster hit her on the head. She looked up and saw a crack in the ceiling and felt a rumbling beneath her.

Mr. Stein was in the doorway, ready to leave. He turned when Chaya screamed.

The van swerved to avoid hitting a Great Dane crossing the road.

"What is it with these animals?" the driver said. "They're all over the place."

Judd saw a flagpole in front of a school rocking back and forth. Road signs swayed, and suddenly the pavement cracked and opened before them.

The driver struggled to keep control of the speeding vehicle, but Judd knew it was too late. They would have to deal with *the wrath of the Lamb.*

Vicki didn't realize what was happening until Mrs. Jenness was already driving over the bridge.

"Stop!" Vicki said. "We have to go back."

"If I have anything to do with it, you're *never* coming back," Mrs. Jenness said.

"You don't understand," Vicki said. "The earthquake. It's happening. We have to get off this bridge."

The top of the bridge swayed first, then the whole structure pitched right, then left. Mrs. Jenness screamed and let go of the wheel. Vicki grabbed it and tried to keep the car steady.

Vicki looked out her window and saw a strange sight. The bridge had tipped so far, she could almost see straight into the water. In the next instant they were tipped the other way, and the water was on Mrs. Jenness's side.

Vicki heard a crash above them. *One of the cables,* she thought. While Mrs. Jenness screamed, Vicki looked around at the windows. She wanted to make sure they were all up.

Phoenix sniffed the air and ran back to the house. So much noise. The ground was moving underneath him.

Sniff.

He had to find the boy. The boy had let him out. Why hadn't he come?

Find the boy. Find the boy. Find the boy.

About the Authors

Jerry B. Jenkins (www.jerryjenkins.com) is the writer of the Left Behind series. He is author of more than one hundred books, of which ten have reached the *New York Times* best-seller list. Former vice president for publishing for the Moody Bible Institute of Chicago, he also served many years as editor of *Moody* magazine and is now Moody's writer-at-large.

His writing has appeared in publications as varied as *Reader's Digest, Parade,* in-flight magazines, and many Christian periodicals. He has written books in four genres: biography, marriage and family, fiction for children, and fiction for adults.

Jenkins's biographies include books with Hank Aaron, Bill Gaither, Luis Palau, Walter Payton, Orel Hershiser, Nolan Ryan, Brett Butler, and Billy Graham, among many others.

Seven of his apocalyptic novels—*Left Behind, Tribulation Force, Nicolae, Soul Harvest, Apollyon, Assassins,* and *The Indwelling*—have appeared on the Christian Booksellers Association's best-selling fiction list and the *Publishers Weekly* religion best-seller list. *Left Behind* was nominated for Book of the Year by the Evangelical Christian Publishers Association in 1997, 1998, and 1999.

As a marriage and family author and speaker, Jenkins has been a frequent guest on Dr. James Dobson's *Focus on the Family* radio program.

Jerry is also the writer of the nationally syndicated sports story comic strip *Gil Thorp,* distributed to newspapers across the United States by Tribune Media Services.

Jerry and his wife, Dianna, live in Colorado.

Limited speaking engagement information available through speaking@jerryjenkins.com.

Dr. Tim LaHaye (www.timlahaye.com), who conceived the idea of fictionalizing an account of the Rapture and the Tribulation, is a noted author, minister, and nationally recognized speaker on Bible prophecy. He is the founder of both Tim LaHaye Ministries and The Pre-Trib Research Center. Presently Dr. LaHaye speaks at many of the major Bible prophecy conferences in the U.S. and Canada, where his nine current prophecy books are very popular.

Dr. LaHaye holds a doctor of ministry degree from Western Theological Seminary and the doctor of literature degree from Liberty University. For twenty-five years he pastored one of the nation's outstanding churches in San Diego, which grew to three locations. It was during that time that he founded two accredited Christian high schools, a Christian school system of ten schools, and Christian Heritage College.

Dr. LaHaye has written over forty books, with over 22 million copies in print in thirty-three languages. He has written books on a wide variety of subjects, such as family life, temperaments, and Bible prophecy. His current fiction works, written with Jerry Jenkins—*Left Behind, Tribulation Force, Nicolae, Soul Harvest, Apollyon, Assassins,* and *The Indwelling*—have all reached number one on the Christian best-seller charts. Other works by Dr. LaHaye are *Spirit-Controlled Temperament; How to Be Happy though Married; Revelation Unveiled; Understanding the Last Days; Rapture under Attack; Are We Living in the End Times?;* and the youth fiction series Left Behind: The Kids.

He is the father of four grown children and grandfather of nine. Snow skiing, waterskiing, motorcycling, golfing, vacationing with family, and jogging are among his leisure activities.

The Future Is Clear

In one shocking moment, millions around the globe disappear. Those left behind face an uncertain future—especially the four kids who now find themselves alone.

Best-selling authors Jerry B. Jenkins and Tim LaHaye present the Rapture and Tribulation through the eyes of four friends—Judd, Vicki, Lionel, and Ryan. As the world falls in around them, they band together to find faith and fight the evil forces that threaten their lives.

#1: The Vanishings Four friends face Earth's last days together.

#2: Second Chance The kids search for the truth.

#3: Through the Flames The kids risk their lives.

#4: Facing the Future The kids prepare for battle.

#5: Nicolae High The Young Trib Force goes back to school.

#6: The Underground The Young Trib Force fights back.

#7: Busted! The Young Trib Force faces pressure.

#8: Death Strike The Young Trib Force faces war.

#9: The Search The struggle to survive.

#10: On the Run The Young Trib Force faces danger.

#11: Into the Storm The search for secret documents.

#12: Earthquake! The Young Trib Force faces disaster.

BOOKS #13 AND #14 COMING SOON!